Praise for

fourth World

"Human-animal genetic manipulation is the motor
that drives this gripping book."
—*The Horn Book*

"[Thompson] weaves some stimulating ideas into this
suspenseful tale and leaves plenty of unanswered
questions for future installments."
—*Kirkus Reviews*

"Readers who enjoy science fiction
with a touch of the adventure/survival genre
will appreciate this first book."
—*VOYA*

"The story is compelling and the questions left open
at the end are intriguing enough to lead
readers . . . into the promised sequel."
—*School Library Journal*

"The novel's agreeable Doctor Doolittle dimension
and shocking conclusion will reap a sizable audience
for the next installment of the Missing Link trilogy."
—*Booklist*

The
MISSING LINK
Trilogy

fourth world

Kate Thompson

BLOOMSBURY

Art and original cover design by James Fraser

Published by Bloomsbury, New York, London, and Berlin
Distributed to the trade by Holtzbrinck Publishers

The Library of Congress has cataloged the hardcover edition as follows:
Thompson, Kate.
Fourth World / Kate Thompson.—1st U.S. ed.
p.   cm. — (Missing link trilogy)
Originally published: Great Britain : The Bodley Head, 2000.
Summary: Fifteen-year-old Christie and his older stepbrother, Danny, travel to
the home and mysterious laboratory of the elder boy's scientist mother, where
they learn a shocking truth about the nature of her experiments.
ISBN 10: 1-58234-650-X • ISBN 13: 978-1-58234-650-2 (hardcover)
[1. Genetic engineering—Fiction. 2. Stepbrothers—Fiction. 3. Animals—Fiction.
4. Scotland—Fiction.] I. Title.
PZ7.T3715965Fo 2005   [Fic]—dc22   2004062367
ISBN 10: 1-58234-897-9 • ISBN 13: 978-1-58234-897-1 (paperback)

Typeset by Hewer Text Ltd, Edinburgh
Printed in the U.S.A.
1 3 5 7 9 10 8 6 4 2

Bloomsbury Publishing, Children's Books, U.S.A.
175 Fifth Avenue, New York, NY 10010

All papers used by Bloomsbury Publishing are natural, recyclable products
made from wood grown in well-managed forests. The manufacturing processes
conform to the environmental regulations of the country of origin.

For Conor

*My thanks to Martha and Morten
and to Fundación*

part
one

one

Everybody in our town had their own ideas about my stepbrother, Danny. Some of them called him disabled, some said he was autistic, and some just referred to him as 'that poor boy'. The truth was that there were only two people who knew what Danny really was. One was his father, who didn't believe it. The other was his mother, who did.

two

I was on the *Titanic*. All my friends were there, and Mom
and Dad; my real dad, not Maurice, and hundreds of other
people. Inside, the lights were blazing, but it was dark
outside the portholes and I knew that Danny was out
there, swimming around in the freezing waters. I looked
down and discovered that I had a fiddle in my hand. When
I looked around, I saw that everyone else had fiddles, too.
On the stage in front of us, Leonardo di Caprio was tapping
a music stand with a conductor's baton.

Tap, tap.

I lifted the fiddle, and at the same time I realised that I
didn't know how to play it.

Tap, tap.

Flames began to spring up among the people. All over
the place. Just from nowhere. I looked at the blank portholes and wondered how to get out; how to join Danny out
there. I couldn't remember how I had got in. Fear began to
clutch at me.

Tap, tap. Tap, tap.

I opened my eyes, delighted to find that I was dreaming. The first light of a dull autumn morning was illuminating my chaotic bedroom. Mom refused to come into it any more. Maurice said it was bad feng shui. At least, I think that's what he said.

Tap, tap.

Leonardo again. Except that it couldn't be. Dreams were mad. Danny swimming. Danny, who was terrified of any stretch of water bigger than the bathtub.

Tap, tap. Rattatap.

The sound was coming from the window. Outside it, in the bluish morning, I could see the dark shape of a bird. As I watched, it turned its head and peered through the glass with a little, bright eye. Then it tapped again with its beak.

I looked at my clock. Just half-past seven. I could have lived with that if it hadn't been Sunday. The bird tapped again. I sat up, hauled one of my pillows out from behind me, and launched it at the window. There was an Action Man and a baked beans money box on the sill and they both went flying, but the bird did as well, and that was what mattered. It gave a funny little squawk as it lifted off, and as I flopped back on to my bed and doubled up my other pillow I laughed. It had sounded just like, 'Cor! Flaming heck!'

I would have to tell Danny about that.

*   *   *

But I forgot. I went back to sleep and when I next saw Danny he didn't put me in the mood to share jokes.

'Come with me to the woods,' he said, lowering himself as carefully as he could on to the end of my bed.

I yelped and pulled my foot out from under him. It was still only eight-thirty.

'Sod off, Danny!' I said.

'Just a little walk,' he said. 'Come on, Christerbie.'

'Christie,' I said. 'Say it properly or don't say it at all.'

Living with Danny was like living with a little brother. Except that he wasn't little. He was big. Fifteen. Two years older than me.

'Come on,' he said. 'Come on.'

He was at his best in the mornings. It was the only time I found him good company. As the day wore on he always lost his clarity and got confused and silly. But it was still Sunday.

'I want a lie-in,' I said. 'It's all right for you. I have to go to school all week.'

I turned over and yanked at my covers, but they were trapped underneath him. I shut my eyes and hoped, but he didn't budge. I could feel his disappointment in the air and I steeled myself against giving in to him.

Everything was so difficult for him. He had been born with some kind of abnormality which made him heavy and clumsy. He had a big, barrel chest and skinny legs which didn't bend quite right, and huge flat feet which always seemed to be in the way. They said he was mentally subnormal, and I suppose they were right, although sometimes, especially in the mornings, I wondered.

When Mom first married Maurice I couldn't believe it. Here I was, not only having to get used to a new father but this freak as well. I hated Mom for marrying Maurice and Maurice for marrying Mom. But most of all I hated Danny. I thought he was just an overgrown toddler, constantly the centre of attention, ruling every waking hour in the new house.

But then, one morning, he came in and sat on my bed, just like he was doing now. I was wide awake that time; still grieving over the change in my life. I told him to go away and leave me alone. But he was clear and lucid, and he said, 'Sorry, Christie. I don't know why I'm like this. I'm some kind of a mistake, aren't I?'

I was shocked. 'No,' I said. 'You're not a mistake. You're just . . .'

'Just what?' he said.

'I don't know,' I said. 'You're just different.'

After that I could never be angry with him any more. I was still angry with Mom and Maurice, but not with Danny.

'Will you come out with me later?' he asked me now.

I groaned. In the early mornings we sometimes managed to get in our walk without meeting anyone else. If we went later, we would be bound to encounter people, and I would have to fend off their attention. 'I want to watch *Top Thirty Hits*,' I said, knowing how feeble I must have sounded. 'And I want to play on the computer, and then there's match on.'

'I hate the telly,' said Danny. 'Real life is better.'

He pointed at the window and I was briefly reminded of the black bird. Then I noticed something else.

'It's raining, anyway,' I said, delighted at the reprieve.

'It's OK,' said Danny. 'We're waterproof.'

'What did he say?' said Maurice, appearing at the door-way in his dressing-gown.

'He thinks he's waterproof,' I said.

'Just as well,' said Maurice. 'It's high time he had a bath.'

Danny loved the bath. He whooped and giggled and followed Maurice off towards the bathroom. As I turned over and snuggled back into the warmth of my lost sleep I remembered the dream. Dreams were mad. Danny swimming. As if.

three

Danny stood at the sitting-room window.

'Look, Christerly,' he said. 'My darling has come back.'

'Your darling?' I said, tearing my eyes away from the match. 'What are you on about, your darling?'

He pointed into the front garden. 'My darling. My darling.'

I usually tried to ignore him, but I had to look.

'See?' he said. 'My darling.'

I joined him at the window and followed the line of his pointing finger, to where a bird like a small black crow sat on the garden wall.

'Starling, Danny,' I said. 'Not "darling". Say "starling".'

'Starling,' said Danny. 'Darling starling.'

'And say "Christie",' I said. 'Not "Christerly".'

'Christerbie,' he said. 'Christmassy, Cricketty, Crinkly.'

'Oh brilliant,' I said. 'And now shut up. I want to watch the match.'

Danny giggled. 'Shut up, smut up, squash up,' he sang, and I knew we were in for trouble.

'Enough, Danny,' I said, with as much threat in my tone as I could muster. 'Don't start now, all right? Just don't start.'

But he had already started, and he was only just getting going. 'Chuff up, Christine, my darling starling, oh my darling saviour starling, follow me up to Scotland.'

He began to dance clumsily about the floor, lurching dangerously close to the television and singing higher and faster. I could have stopped him if I'd had the patience, but he was really annoying me, and I was slipping back into the familiar resentment that ruled my new life.

'Mom!' I shouted. 'Mom! Do something about Danny, will you!'

I knew it wasn't really her problem, either, though she did her best to cope. But I wasn't going to call my step-father. It would have been an admission of a relationship that I still refused to acknowledge.

He came in, anyway.

Danny was still singing, saluting the window and flapping his arms like a grotesque bird-man. 'Fly away with me, darling starling. Fly high in the sky, bye-bye.'

'He's all right, Christie,' said Maurice. 'He's only singing.'

'And I'm only trying to watch the blasted match, aren't I?'

Danny picked up on the tension, and his voice slid up the scale. He started whooping and wailing, higher than a kite, nutty as a fruitcake.

'All right, Danny,' said Maurice, but his tone suggested that he knew it was hopeless, that Danny would get higher and higher until he ended up shouting and crying and throwing a tantrum. He was too big now for his father to restrain him, and if he couldn't be persuaded to calm down it often ended with Maurice having to give him a sedative. Either that or he would hyperventilate and pass out. I had discovered my own way of dealing with him, but it was my secret. Knowing it, and keeping it to myself, made me feel powerful. I might look normal on the outside, but I had hidden powers. I was a clandestine magician. One day I might tell them, but not yet. I wasn't ready to let Maurice off the hook.

Instead I stormed out, leaving the television to compete with Danny's chaos.

Mom was standing in the kitchen, looking anxious. She stroked my hair apologetically, but I wriggled away.

'I'm going round to Matty's for a game of Warhammer,' I said.

Mom nodded. 'OK.'

Matty's house was about a mile away. 'Can I have a lift?' I asked.

'You're joking, aren't you?' said Mom.

'No. Why?'

'Hasn't it sunk in on you yet?' she said. 'Haven't you noticed that we've had petrol rationing for six weeks now?'

I did know, of course. It was all over the news all the time. Boring. I suppose it didn't really affect me all that much. I always cycled to school and I didn't go out much otherwise. And if we didn't have the obligatory weekend outings to the relatives it was a relief, not a hardship. I thought it was just another of those endless 'adult' problems that they seemed to like complaining about. So when Mom refused me a lift that day, I just got sulky and said I wouldn't go. Then, when that produced no results, I changed my mind and decided to walk.

The black bird was sitting on the garden gate when I went out. I wouldn't have noticed it, except that it didn't fly away as I approached. It put its head on one side and stared at me with a shrewd brown eye. I remembered that it had been at my window.

'Shoo!' I said, reaching for the latch.

'Shoo yourself,' said the bird. 'Are you Danny?'

Mom was calling me from the front door. 'What time will you be back?'

I tore my eyes from the bird and turned to her, but I couldn't answer.

'Not later than nine, you hear?' she said.

I promised and turned back to the gate. But the bird had gone.

I was hearing things, that was all.

four

At about half-past ten that night, just about the time when I was walking home from Matty Duignan's house, another part of this story was beginning somewhere else. About a hundred and eighty miles away. In Dublin.

In the dark lanes which ran parallel to Grafton Street, the ISPCA dog wardens were working. They were trying to round up a stray; a black and white sheepdog that had been hanging around the area for some time. But he was proving, as ever, elusive.

They came across him raiding the bins at the back of a Chinese restaurant. The driver stopped the van and quietly the two men got out. The dog was trying to reach some scraps in the bottom of an overturned bin, and his head was deep inside it. The first he knew of the presence of the dog wardens was the feel of a heavily gloved hand taking hold of the scruff of his neck.

Quicker than thought, the dog snaked round and wrenched free of the clumsy hand. His head missed the waiting choke chain by a hair's breadth, and before the wardens could make another grab he was hurtling down the street and away.

The two men threw mouthfuls of curses after him and leapt back into their van. In all their years in the business they had never come across a dog like him. He seemed friendly and intelligent, and on the first couple of occasions that they had got close to him, he had fawned and wagged his tail and smiled at them. But at a safe distance. No matter how sweetly they spoke to him or what delightful titbits they offered, they could not tempt him to come within reach. This evening was the first time that either of them had touched him.

They sped after him, as fast as was safe in the narrow lanes. At a crossroads they stopped and just caught sight of his tail as he slipped round the corner of the next junction. But by the time they got there, the dog was nowhere to be seen. Slowly they cruised the street, peering behind parked cars and crawling past skips and bins. A couple came out of the pub, but apart from them the only living thing they could see was a homeless girl huddled in blankets at the rear doorway of a shopping arcade.

'Poor kid,' she heard one of them say, as they drove on by.

The girl made a V-sign with her fingers after the van. Then she laughed.

'You're tickling me!'

The dog scrambled out from the tent the girl had made with her knees. He licked her face.

'Stop, stop!' she shouted, pushing him away, then changing her mind and pulling him back. She held him tight against her and wrapped her arms around him. Bony ribs knocked against bony ribs.

'You're even skinnier than I am,' said the girl.

'I'm not,' said the dog.

The girl cast her mind back across the day. She had met up with Mick in Stephen's Green in the afternoon, but she was sure he hadn't given her anything. In fact, she hadn't taken any kind of drugs since the time she had landed up in hospital last Christmas. She didn't even like to think about that.

'I like you,' said the dog.

Tina wondered if it was a flashback. She knew that it could happen; that the drug experience could return months, or even years, later.

'We're in the same boat,' said the dog.

Maybe it was that bottle of cider she had shared with Mick and Ronan yesterday. It had made her feel a bit peculiar, all right.

'I'm Oggy,' said the dog. 'I'm lost as well.'

'I'm not lost,' said Tina.

'Oh,' said Oggy. 'Does that mean that I'm found?'

A tall, rangy boy was shuffling along the street. The dog wavered for a moment, thinking about running, but the girl put a kind hand on his head and he slumped against her gratefully.

' 'Lo, Mick,' she said.

' 'Lo, Tina G,' said the boy. 'Anything happening?'

'Yeah,' said Tina. 'This dog has been talking to me.'

'Great, great,' said Mick. 'Nice dog.'

'Yeah, nice dog,' said Tina. 'But he's been talking to me, Mick. I mean, speaking, like.'

'That's great, Tina. I mean, that's really cool.'

'His name is Oggy,' said Tina. 'Why don't you speak to Mick, Oggy?'

Oggy wagged his tail and licked her face.

'Go on,' she said. 'Talk to him like you talked to me.'

Oggy lifted a paw on to Tina's knee, then rolled over on to his back and waved all four feet in the air.

'Nice dog,' said Mick.

'Talk to him, Oggy,' Tina pointed at Mick. 'Go on. Talk to him.'

Oggy got up and took two steps towards Mick, then growled menacingly.

'Ah, no, it's cool,' said Mick, backing off. 'I believe you.'

'Are you stupid or what?' said Tina to the dog.

'See you around,' said Mick, walking rapidly away down the street. Oggy watched him go, then returned to Tina's side and licked her face ecstatically.

'I like you!' he said.

five

Mom gave me a hard time about coming home late, and I went upstairs in a huff. The door to Danny's room was open. I looked in.

He was in bed, already drowsy from the sleeping pill that he had to take every night. I went in and sat down on the chair beside him.

'All right, Danny?'

'All right, Christie.'

His *banky*, the grubby woollen blanket that he carried with him everywhere, was draped over the rest of his bedclothes. He clutched at the corner of it and dragged it closer to his cheek.

'Do you like my mom, Danny?' I asked.

He giggled and nodded. He loved everyone, Danny did. He was always happy, except when he got into a tizzy and went over the top.

'You like my mom,' he said.

'I don't really know her,' I said.

Danny's eyelids began to close and I stayed quiet, thinking about his mother, Maggie. She had come to see him once, soon after Mom and Maurice got married. She had taken him out for a walk in the woods, and I had waited at home, watching TV. Maurice was clearly worried; kept looking at his watch and pacing round the room. It was irritating.

'What's up with you?' I said, and my tone made Mom flinch.

'I just don't trust her, that's all,' he said.

'Why?' I said. 'What do you think she's going to do?'

Maurice shrugged. 'She's not like you and me, Christie. That woman is a law unto herself. There's no knowing what she might get up to.'

I turned back to the TV, but the ads were on.

'Why does Danny live with you, anyway?' I asked. 'Why doesn't he live with her?'

'It's a long story,' said Maurice, glancing at Mom in a conspiratorial sort of way. 'Danny's mother isn't really fit to look after a child. He has lived with me since he was a baby.'

'She looks all right to me,' I said.

'She is all right,' said Mom. 'It's just that she . . . well . . . she attaches more importance to her work than . . .'

Maurice was looking at her in a warning kind of way.

It made me determined to push on. 'What kind of work does she do?'

'She's a scientist,' said Maurice.

'Cool,' I said, delighted to be able to oppose him in yet another matter. 'What kind of scientist?'

'A mad one,' he said.

I laughed but he didn't, and there was a darkness in his expression that persuaded me not to press on any further.

When Danny and Maggie came back, we sat around in the kitchen and drank tea and ate ham sandwiches. She was a bit mad-looking, I suppose, with wild, wind-blown hair and a fresh look to her skin, as though she spent most of her life striding through storms. I thought she was beautiful, not in a sexy way, but kind of magical and powerful. I couldn't help watching her, wondering what kind of science she worked at. After a while, she told me there were presents for Danny and me in a bag in the sitting-room, and asked if I'd take Danny out to open them.

I did. There were the obligatory Scottish things; Edinburgh rock and shortbread, but the other things were cool: a solar clock you could make yourself for Danny, and a book for me called *Catastrophe Theory*.

I went in to say thanks and found myself in the middle of one of those storms I had imagined.

'No way!' Maurice was saying. 'Not in a million years!'

'He's my son, Maurice,' said Maggie. 'Did it never occur to you that he might be better off with me?'

'Better off with you? That's a joke! After what you did to him?'

They all looked at me, then, and I knew that there was

something private; something I wasn't to know. Then Maggie said, more quietly, 'I know him, Maurice. I know what he is. I can help him, don't you see?'

'Help him?' said Maurice, his anger driving him close to apoplexy. 'Help him?'

Mom made a face at me and I went out again, to where Danny was happily unpacking the pieces of the solar clock. Behind me the row went on and on, until eventually Maggie left. She came to say goodbye to us; Danny wept and wept, and when she went out he started to go over the top and Maurice had to come and take him away. I watched Maggie sweeping down the garden path and walking along the street towards the bus station. I wished I could go with her.

Danny's eyes shot open again.

'Open my window, Christie,' he said.

I opened it, just a crack.

'You like my mother,' he went on.

'I told you, Danny. I don't know her.'

He shook his head. 'When we go to Scotland,' he said. 'Watch out for my darling.' As he slipped over the edge of sleep he mumbled again. 'You like her.'

When I went downstairs, the news was on the television. I played with the Gameboy and didn't really listen, but I knew there was something about the oil crisis worsening. Mom shook her head a lot and made worried noises, but Maurice said it would never happen; they wouldn't allow it.

Whatever 'it' was.

After the news Mom and Maurice went to bed, but I stayed up to watch *Aliens 3*. Mom said she didn't like me watching things like that, but Maurice said boys needed adventure, and these days the only way they could get it was by watching it on TV.

Afterwards I wished I had listened to Mom. The film had given me the creeps and I couldn't sleep. I found myself thinking about Maggie again, and about something else that had happened on the day she came to see Danny. I had finished off some homework and I went down to the kitchen to get some tea. Danny was already asleep, and

Mom and Maurice were sitting at the table. I was in my socks. They didn't hear me come down.

Mom was saying, 'But she must have some rights to him. In law, I mean. If she decided to push it.'

'She won't do that,' said Maurice. 'She wouldn't dare. She knows I could shop her tomorrow if I had half a mind.'

I stayed still, breathing slowly and silently. There was a pause, and then Mom said, 'What do you mean, "shop her"?'

There was a longer pause, and I could hear Maurice moving restlessly. Then he said, 'She's doing things up there that are . . . well . . . not entirely legal.'

'What sort of things?' said Mom.

There was another pause, and then Maurice said, 'Is that you, Christie?'

I stepped into the kitchen. 'What's not legal?' I said.

But Maurice was as silent as an egg.

'Fine,' I said. 'Be like that.'

seven

A candle was flickering in my room; one of those tiny little night-light things. I could see Danny peering down at me and, sitting on top of my bedside lamp, so was the black bird.

I experienced that sudden, overwhelming terror that happens in dreams, just before you wake. I sat up, shrinking away until my back met the wall, waiting for that blessed moment when I would open my eyes on to reality; mundane and secure. But it didn't come.

'Darling,' said Danny. 'My darling has come.'

I had a sudden image of the bird flying into my face, its wings flapping, its long, pointed beak probing my eye sockets.

'Say hello,' said Danny, sounding groggy, a bit like Boris Karloff, as he battled with the sedative still lingering in his bloodstream. 'Say hello, Darling.'

'Hello,' said the bird.

'Hello,' I said, suddenly enchanted.

'I told you she would come,' said Danny. 'I told you to

watch out for my darling. You have to come with us, Christie. I can't go without you.'

'Go where?' I said, but I was still waiting for the dream to be over.

'Scotland,' said Danny. 'To Mother. The darling will bring us.'

I noticed that Danny had got himself dressed. He was holding the corner of his *banky*, which streamed out on the floor behind him.

'Your mother's mad,' I said. 'And so are you.'

'She told me,' said Danny. 'She told me someone would come to get us. She gave me this.'

He opened his fist and revealed a fat wad of notes. I sat up on the edge of the bed and tried to get a better look. But at that moment the bird rose up from the lamp and flitted towards the door, its wings whirring like a bat in the small bedroom. I flinched away, then looked up again. The starling was gone, and Danny was lumbering after it on unsteady legs, dragging the stupid old blanket behind him.

'Danny!' I called, but softly, aware that the rest of the household was asleep. Aware, even though I didn't know it, that what was happening was not for the adult world to know.

He ignored me, and I heard him sliding down the stairs, on his bum, as usual.

I flopped back on to the bed, trying to figure out what was going on, still hoping that it might be a dream. I had

25

almost succeeded when I heard the soft click of the front door opening, and that little whir of wings again, down in the front hall.

I should have woken Mom and Maurice. If I had, none of it would have happened. We would have been back in bed within half an hour, Danny doped up again, the bird chased outside where it belonged, back in the darkness. But I didn't do it. Maybe because it was all so strange and secret. Maybe because I was still angry with Maurice. I don't know. But what I did do was jump out of bed, drag my jeans and jumper on over my pyjamas, and stuff my bare feet into my boots. I slipped down the stairs commando style; swift and silent, and grabbed my jacket off the peg on the wall.

And there I was. Out in the pre-dawn darkness, breathing frosty plumes into the air.

Danny was a good distance down the street, shuffling along in his penguin gait towards the main road. I could just make out the quick dart of the starling ahead of him as it passed beneath a street lamp.

I turned back towards the house. I could still wake them. Or I could have, if I hadn't just closed the front door behind me and locked us both out. I'd have to bang like hell now to get them up. Better to catch Danny first.

He was already at the end of the street, waving his arms in some kind of weird delight as he wobbled along. If a squad car passed he'd be in the nick before he could blink. I bent and laced my boots, then set out after him.

eight

By the time I got to the end of the street, Danny was away down the main road, moving in a cumbersome dance along the footpath. He was going surprisingly fast, and the starling was darting around above his head, in and out of the street lights. I caught them up and nipped round to stand in front of Danny. He sidestepped and pushed past me, his face split by an enormous grin.

The exercise was clearing the sedative from his system.

'Going on the bus, Christie,' he said, flashing the roll of notes in front of my face. 'Going to Scotland.'

'No way, Danny,' I said, trying to get in front of him again.

He laughed delightedly and swung the filthy blanket at me, blinding me and knocking me off balance. I grabbed it and hauled hard, swinging him round to face me. At last he stopped, and for a moment there was fear in his eyes.

'Come on, Crispy.'

My heart sank. I had been living with him for six months

now, and I knew the warning signs. If he flipped now, here in the dark empty streets, I wouldn't know what to do. My secret trick might work, but it might not.

I glanced back the way we had come, considering the possibility of racing back for Maurice. But we were much too far from home. By the time I got there and coaxed Maurice out of bed, Danny could be miles away, trundling happily towards his fantasy Scotland.

'Listen, Danny,' I said. 'It's OK. I'll go to Scotland with you. But not now, all right? It's not a good time.'

'It's a perfect time,' said a little piping voice from a branch behind my shoulder.

I turned round. The starling was sitting there, glaring at me, sinister as a little raven in the gloom.

I couldn't get my head around what I was hearing. Danny laughed and whooped, and started to shamble off again, swinging his blanket up around his chest like a poncho.

'No, Danny!'

I ran after him and tried to stop him again, but his eyes had that wild look and he had started to gulp air. He was giggling and singing, and the pitch of his voice was rising. I was in for trouble.

'Steady down, now,' I said. 'Come on, I tell you what, I'll walk you to the bus stop, all right? But you have to slow down. You have to hold your breath.'

Danny nodded and linked his arm into mine and we

walked on, the bird ahead and behind like a tiny shadow. Danny could hold his breath for longer than anyone I had ever met. He seemed to be able to hold his breath for longer than was humanly possible. I had timed him once for more than six minutes, and he wasn't blue or anything.

We had discovered it by accident, just playing games, a kind of contest. But I soon realised that after his marathon sessions Danny was always calmer, sometimes almost normal. So once or twice, when he looked like he was getting over-excited, I had tried it out; getting him to hold his breath and see what happened. It had worked. He had held and held and held, and by the time he let go, the crisis would have passed. That was my secret; the thing I never told Maurice or Mom. The little bit of power I held in the family circle.

I watched him now as we walked. I watched him as closely as I could, convinced that he must have some way of cheating. But I couldn't see it. He wasn't taking tiny quick ones, and he wasn't letting anything in or out, even slowly.

And it was working. I could see the lucidity returning to his eyes. I hoped that by the time he was finished holding I'd be able to talk some sense into him.

But he held all the way to the bus station. I couldn't believe it. I didn't have a watch so I couldn't time him, but it must have been more like seven minutes than five. When we got there I couldn't believe he was still standing, let alone walking. But what mattered was that my trick had worked. He was sane and calm, and now he might listen. The early coach to Dublin was standing ready, but for some reason no one had been allowed to get on yet, and quite a queue had formed. Danny moved forward to join it, but I pulled him away and pinned him against the wall.

'Now, Danny,' I said, trying to sound brotherly and clever; sounding like a teacher instead. 'I don't think this is a great idea, not just now. What do you think?'

In answer he shoved the fistful of notes into my hand and said, 'You buy the tickets, Christie.'

'I will, Danny,' I said. 'But I don't think this is the best bus to go on, do you?'

'Yes,' said Danny. 'Best bus.'

'But this is the Dublin bus,' I said. 'It's not the Scotland bus.'

A shadow of doubt crossed Danny's face, but then his face brightened again.

'Dublin first,' he said. 'Then the boat. Then Scotland.'

He pushed away from me and made to join the line. Everyone turned and looked at Danny, and then pretended that they weren't looking, which was worse. But, unusually, no one looked back. There was a nervous intensity about the people in the queue and I tuned in to a nearby conversation.

'It's on account of the oil crisis,' a smartly dressed woman was saying to a young man with a briefcase. 'It's all getting much worse, you know. There's talk of all kinds of emergencies happening. The bus might not run at all.'

I tried to hide my relief. That would have been perfect as far as I was concerned. It would avoid the blow-up that was now beginning to seem inevitable.

'Do you hear that, Danny?' I said. 'The bus might not be going at all.'

'We can walk,' said Danny.

I laughed, but I wasn't so sure that he was joking. I had seen him in action before. If he made up his mind to do something, nothing short of sedatives would stop him.

Just then a driver broke away from a blue-uniformed gathering by the office and came over to our bus.

'We'll bring you to Dublin,' he announced, 'but you'll have to understand that we can't guarantee any buses coming back. We haven't got a directive from the minister, yet. But any bus could be the last.'

People nodded and murmured and glanced at each other, but not at us.

'So if you don't have to travel, we advise you not to, all right?'

One or two dropped out of the queue and walked away, presumably going home, but the others tightened up the line, expressing their mutual decision to travel. The driver opened the bus door and got into his seat.

I tried to draw Danny aside, but he had begun to press forward with the other travellers.

'Now wait, Danny,' I said. 'Let's talk about this some more.'

'No talking,' said Danny. 'Going to Scotland.'

'Oh, God,' I said. What was I going to do now? If I stopped him from getting on the bus he'd throw an out-and-out wobbler. There was no doubt about that. And he wouldn't do any breath-holding for me, either. Not if I was thwarting him. I wished I had woken Maurice.

The others were nearly all on the bus. We were at the back, and I was still trying to work out a last minute stroke of genius when the starling landed on my shoulder. I jumped and shook it off, but it came back again, clinging on to the fabric of my jacket with sharp claws.

'Put me in your pocket, Christie,' it said. 'Then get on the bus.'

nine

I stared straight ahead of me, completely gobsmacked. No matter how I tried, I couldn't make the starling's speech fit into my version of reality. My mind jumped through hoops. It was a toy, a clever machine. But it wasn't. It had just learned a few words, like a parrot. But it hadn't. There was a magician around, throwing her voice. I looked around. There wasn't. But while I was standing there trying to figure it out, this crazy twist of fate was continuing to work on me. Because Danny was already clambering aboard the bus, pointing me out to the driver, shuffling up between the rows of seats.

I was seeing it all but I couldn't make sense of it.

'In your pocket, Christie,' said the starling.

'Are you getting on or what?' called the bus driver, revving the huge engine.

I would never get Danny off that bus now. Not without the wobbler of a lifetime. I had a sudden vision of the bus in chaos, and of me dragging him by the feet, backwards down the steps on to the footpath. I did the only thing I could. I stepped forward.

As I did so, the starling fluttered madly at the breast of my jacket, and I pulled open the flap and let her into the big poacher's pocket in the lining. By the time I was finished I was on the bus, the driver was giving me strange looks, and I was staring at the bundle of notes, all sweaty in my fist.

A shock ran through me. The notes were a joke, some sort of toy money. I was about ready to crack.

'Dublin, is it?' said the driver, losing patience. I nodded, scrabbling at the money, opening the roll. In the middle, to my relief, were the familiar Irish notes: fives, tens, twenties. I handed one over, and the driver printed out the tickets and counted out my change. In my pocket I could feel the starling moving around. Something dropped on to the floor beside my foot. A stub of a pencil. Then more things: an old chocolate wrapper, a broken Warhammer piece, an ice-lolly stick. The bird was making herself comfortable. I didn't pick them up, and hoped that no one had noticed.

Danny had found a seat at the back. I sat down beside him and inspected the funny money. It was sterling; some English and some Scottish.

It was for real, then. Danny's mother had given him this money. Somehow or other, she really did expect him to make his way to her, in Scotland. And somehow or other, I had allowed myself to get dragged into it.

Danny was giggling. 'Yay, yay. Going to Scotland,' he said.

I smiled to humour him. We were stuck as far as Dublin, anyway. But I had no intention whatsoever of going any further.

part
two

As the sun rose, Oggy and Tina were just waking up in their doorway. Oggy gazed at Tina with that eternally devoted look that dogs have, but Tina looked back with suspicion.

'I had a funny dream about you,' she said.

'Did you?' said Oggy.

'Hmm,' said Tina. 'It wasn't a dream.'

The cleaners arrived with the keys to the shopping centre.

'How's it going, Tina?' said one.

'Got any fags?' said Tina.

'Get yourself a chimney if you want to smoke,' said one of the others.

'Yeah,' said another. 'And a house to go with it.'

'Thanks,' said Tina. 'Bite her, Oggy.'

But Oggy didn't. When the women had gone inside and locked the door behind them again, he said, 'They weren't so bad. They were only messing.'

'They weren't,' said Tina. 'I hate them.'

'Oh. Don't hate them,' said Oggy.

'I hate everybody,' said Tina, staring into space. 'Everybody except you.'

Oggy licked her face then looked back towards the street and sniffed the air. The smell of frying was drifting around them from an early morning café somewhere nearby.

'What do you do for breakfast round here?' said Oggy.

'Breakfast?' said Tina. 'What breakfast?'

'Pity about you,' said Oggy, and set off at a trot along the street.

two

Despite his delight at being on the bus, Danny was exhausted from battling with the sedative, and went out like a light as soon as we started to move. He was slumped against the window and every time we went over a bump his head rattled against it. I managed to drag a bit of his *banky* out of his clutches and stuff it under his head. It didn't make any difference to him but it did, at least, stop people from staring.

I was too hot in my jacket but I couldn't take it off because of Darling, who also seemed to have gone to sleep. Now that the excitement of the moment had passed I was beginning to get frightened again. What would Mom and Maurice do when they found we were missing? Would they go searching the fields behind our street and the woods beyond? Would they think something awful had happened? Would they call in the police?

And the thoughts that came after that were even scarier. Because what was happening couldn't be real. I was in a bus with my loopy stepbrother, heading towards some unknown place where his mother might, or might not, be waiting for us. I tried to remember what I knew about her, but it wasn't much. She was rich, Maurice said, as well as mad. She had come into some colossal inheritance from some American relation and she and Maurice had set up home in Scotland, where they worked together on some kind of research. But then it was confused. Something had happened to Danny. Maurice had taken him away from his mother and gone back to live in Ireland. What was it Maurice had said? Her crazy dreams mattered more to her than what was real.

The words spooked me. Because now, here on this trundling bus, dreams were becoming real. There was a talking starling in my pocket. The impossible was happening. If I wasn't mad then the world was, and I didn't know which was worse.

three

Oggy, meanwhile, had found a little shop doing a strong trade in morning papers. He sat at the door as though he were waiting for his owner, and if anyone noticed him they said things like, 'Ah, how sweet' and 'What a good dog'.

It was the ideal shop for Oggy. The bread was near the door on a tall, narrow set of shelves. It was only a question of being patient and picking his moment. It came when a bit of a queue developed at the counter and there was no one near the door. Oggy was in and out like a flash, and he didn't wait around to find out if he had been seen.

'You're a star,' said Tina, as they shared the loaf. 'I thought you'd run out on me.'

Oggy's mouth was full and he didn't reply. Besides, there were people around now, and it was too risky.

'Not talking to me, eh?' said Tina. Oggy gave her face a crumb-sticky lick.

'Eeugh!' said Tina. 'Gerrroff!'

A man with a suit came up to the door with a bunch of keys.

'Clear off, now,' he said. 'We're opening for business.'

'I'll set my dog on you,' said Tina.

'Will you?' said the man. 'I'll set the police on you, so.'

Tina packed up the last of the loaf and moved a couple of feet away from the door. Then she rummaged around in her big cloth bag and pulled out a large piece of rain-softened cardboard. It had been torn unevenly from a box, and on one side was printed 'Kello Ri Kri'. On the other side, Tina had written: 'I Am Homeless Please Help'. As Oggy watched, she found a stubby pencil, crossed out 'I Am' and scratched in 'We Are'.

'There!' she said, holding it up for Oggy to see. He looked around in embarrassment and scratched his ear with a hind leg.

'Come on,' said Tina. 'Let's go and see what we can get.'

four

I fell asleep, too, and strange bits of dreams came and went, but none of them were stranger than waking and discovering that it was all still happening. As we pulled into Busaras, I woke Danny. He was calm and clear-headed.

'Oh,' he said, his face lighting up with pleasure. 'We're here.'

Sometimes I envied his carefree attitude towards life. At his best, Danny was probably the happiest person I had ever come across. I wished I could share his excitement, but I couldn't. All I could think about was how to get to a phone and call Maurice without giving the game away and causing a tantrum.

As we waited for everyone to get off the bus, Darling began to stir in my pocket. I was surprised to find that I was glad. She had been ominously still.

'Can I come out?' she whispered.

'Not yet,' I whispered back. 'In a while.'

But as soon as I got off the bus I wished I had let her out. Because the station was bedlam. There were people milling about everywhere, bumping and jostling carelessly, crowding around the departure gates, mobbing the information desk and the ticket counters. Anyone in uniform was surrounded by anxious passengers, but no one, it seemed, was going anywhere.

I locked my elbow up as a shield for Darling, but I couldn't help Danny, who was having serious difficulty keeping his balance.

'Let's get out of here,' I said.

As we made slow, painful progress towards the exit doors, a voice came over a loudspeaker above our heads: 'THIS IS AN ANNOUNCEMENT ON BEHALF OF BUS EIREANN. THERE WILL BE NO BUSES, REPEAT, NO BUSES, UNTIL FURTHER NOTICE. WE ARE AWAITING INSTRUCTIONS FROM CENTRAL GOVERNMENT IN RELATION TO FUEL SUPPLIES FOR PUBLIC TRANSPORT. UNTIL SUCH TIME THERE WILL BE NO BUSES. REPEAT. NO BUSES.'

The crowds at the doors were the worst. My warding elbow earned me some dirty looks but it served its purpose. When I finally broke free of the throng and walked away from the building, I heard Darling say, 'Cor, flaming hell. What's going on?'

I let her out. She flew on to the roof rack of a nearby van and fluffed and fluttered so vigorously that she nearly shook herself off it. She had just succeeded in getting her feathers back in order when Danny caught up with us.

'No more buses,' he said.

'I gathered that.'

'We'll have to walk to Dun Laoghaire, so,' he said.

'What?'

I was amazed that Danny knew where to go. His mother must have briefed him well. I had to play for time.

'Right, so, Danny,' I said. 'But let's take a break first, eh? Get some breakfast?'

He nodded enthusiastically, and I peered back through the crowds into the bus station. There was a coffee shop there, but it was crammed with people standing with sandwiches or lining up at the counter. What was more, the queues for the public phones were a mile long. This latest development in the fuel crisis had thrown everyone's lives out of kilter. Wherever these people were planning to go; home, or work, or holidays; they weren't going there now. I went back outside and, suddenly, all my anxieties were overwhelmed by a single urgency. I really did need to eat.

'Come on, Danny,' I said. 'Let's find a café.'

In fact it was nearer to lunch time, but the little café we found did an all-day breakfast and it was just what I wanted. Darling agreed to wait outside on the condition that we save her a few toast crusts dipped in tea. As I walked into the warm interior of the café, I was amazed to realise that I had begun to relate to the talking bird as though it was the most natural thing in the world.

five

Tina and Oggy were sitting on O'Connell Bridge. They were sharing a grubby blanket to keep out the rain, and the sight of them huddled together behind their homeless notice was having the right effect on the passing crowds.

Tina pocketed a few of the gathered coins. 'I'm keeping you,' she said to Oggy. 'You're good luck.'

Oggy put his nose to her ear and whispered into it. 'I'm keeping you, too.'

Together they watched the pairs of passing feet until one of them stopped, and then another.

'Hey, Tina G,' said Mick.

'Hey, Mick,' said Tina. 'Hey, Ronan.'

'Is that the talking dog?' asked Ronan, with a sniffling giggle. Each of the lads had a polystyrene take-away cup in his hand, but Tina guessed they weren't drinking coffee.

'What's he saying today?' said Ronan, taking a swig and swaying, slightly.

'Bow wow,' said Tina. 'What do you think?'

Ronan roared with laughter. 'Bow wow,' he squawked.

'That's a good one!' He bent down and pushed his face into Oggy's. 'Bow wow, doggy,' he yelled. 'Bow wow wow.'

Oggy snarled and Ronan snarled back. He was a basket case at the best of times, and ten times worse when he was drinking.

'Give us a couple of quid, Tina,' said Mick.

Tina fished out a handful of small coins and handed them over. It was an unwritten rule among the homeless kids, and Mick would always do the same for Tina if he could. But Ronan wasn't finished. He grabbed the blanket and wrenched it off them.

'Come out and play, doggy. Bow wow.'

Oggy barked. Mick took Ronan's arm and tried to lead him away.

'Come on, Rone.' He jangled the coins. 'Want some chips?'

'Oh, yeah, cool,' said Ronan. 'Chips, yeah.'

As Mick steered him away towards O'Connell Street, Oggy stepped away from Tina and gave a few sharp barks at the departing boys.

And that was when Darling spotted him.

She had got bored with waiting for me and Danny and was entertaining herself by teasing the seabirds who wheeled above the river. Like all starlings she was a brilliant mimic, and she was dodging in and out among the gulls, imitating their mournful cries.

When she first saw Oggy she couldn't believe it, and came whirring down to land on the parapet of the bridge for a closer look. Tina heard the whistle she gave at the same time as Oggy did. It went whooshing up the scale and then slid down again more slowly, like someone on a roller coaster shouting: *wheeeeeeee!*

Tina thought it was a firework, left over from Halloween. Then Oggy went haywire. He flung himself at the parapet and Tina saw a black bird lift off and hover just above his head, making funny clackety ratchety noises and more of those ecstatic whoops. People on the pavement stopped to stare, and an astonished lorry driver almost crunched into the car ahead.

The dog was bounding and snapping at the bird, which kept just inches above his lethal jaws. Round and around they twisted in a delirium of excitement and then, quite suddenly, the dog sat down and the bird settled on his head.

Every eye on the bridge was upon them and, when they realised that, they slipped off around the end of the bridge and along the quayside, leaving Tina calling uselessly after her dog.

six

I finished my breakfast ages before Danny, and I hit on a ruse to give him the slip for a few minutes.

'I'm just taking these crusts out to Darling,' I said. 'Don't move now, you hear?'

'Won't move,' he said, through a mouthful of black pudding.

I dunked the crusts in tea and slipped out into the bustling Dublin day. A few yards down the quayside I could see a little block of phone boxes, but there was no sign of Darling. I deposited the sloppy bread on the river wall and scooted down to the phones.

Maurice picked up on the first ring. He sounded frantic.

'Where the hell are you?' he said.

I was shocked by his tone, and what I meant to say went out of my head. 'Out of town,' was what came out.

'What do you mean, out of town?' Maurice said. 'Where out of town? What the hell do you think you're playing at?'

'We're fine, Maurice. We're . . .'

'You're not fine!' He was yelling now, and I could hear

Mom in the background trying to steady him. But he went on at the same pitch. 'I can't understand why you're doing this, Christie! I thought you were responsible. I never should have trusted you!'

I couldn't believe it. My sense of well-being evaporated, and my residual anger against Maurice surfaced and obliterated everything else in my mind. Or almost everything. Into the red rage an image arose, of Danny's mother striding away down our street, her back straight and strong; a powerful, mysterious being.

There was an ominous pause, then Maurice said, 'Christie, listen to me.' His voice was quieter now, but there was a dreadful urgency in it. 'You won't be able to manage Danny, don't you realise that? He needs me. He needs his medication.'

But Maurice had already made his bed, and I was going to make sure that he lay in it.

I put the phone down. I hung up on Maurice and Mom, left them to their cosy togetherness, turned my back on the life I never wanted and looked out on to the Dublin streets and my unknown, unknowable future.

As I went back into the café and paid for our breakfasts, I experienced a rush of excitement. Like suddenly getting the hang of one of those racing-car video games, I had the sensation of being in control; of knowing I was on the right track after all; of embracing my fate and looking forward to what it might bring.

Danny knocked the milk jug off the table as he struggled to get up, but it didn't break.

'You're all right,' said the waitress, handing over my change. Magnanimously, I dropped a pound coin into the TIPS jar, then followed Danny out into the street.

'Right,' I said to him. 'Next stop, Dun Laoghaire.'

Danny was nervous of the river, and I was careful to keep him on the town side of the road, well away from it. There was no sign of Darling, but as we passed beside the phone boxes she came whirring in and alighted on the river wall. Two men were passing by and she fluttered away again until they were safely out of earshot. Then she returned.

'I've found Oggy,' she whistled. 'Come on, come on!'

'Oggy?' I said. 'Who's Oggy?'

'Dog,' said Danny.

'He was supposed to collect you a couple of weeks ago,' said Darling. 'But he got lost. Couldn't remember the map. Bird brain!'

Danny laughed, a mad, tuneless sound against the tuneless buzz of traffic. 'Where is he?' he said.

'Not far,' said Darling. 'I'll show you.'

She hopped on to a parked Jeep a little way ahead and we began to follow. 'Only one problem, though,' she said, as we came up to her.

'What's that?' I asked.

Darling cocked her head and looked at me mischie-vously. 'He's picked up a stray,' she said.

eight

I took a dislike to Tina the first moment I saw her. As we approached her she glared at us with undisguised hostility. It was too busy for introductions on the bridge, and Darling and Oggy started to lead us to somewhere quieter. Tina hung back and I hoped she wouldn't come, but Oggy wouldn't go without her. He went back and whined at her, and put his head to one side, and made cute doggy gestures. I wasn't so sure that I liked him, either.

Tina gathered up her sign and her bag. As we walked up Westmoreland Street on our way to Stephen's Green I decided to try and be friendly.

'Would you say there are less cars about?'

She was chewing some kind of gum and she went to great trouble to blow an ugly grey bubble before she answered me.

'Less cars than what?'

I shrugged. 'Less cars than yesterday?'

Tina looked around, but if she was in agreement with me she wasn't about to admit it.

'What if there is?' she said.

'Just . . . you know. The fuel crisis,' I said. She looked blank, and I went on, 'There's no oil. The war in the Gulf. All the wells are burning. Anybody who has oil is hanging on to it, waiting for the price to go up. Brinksmanship, you know?'

I was surprised at myself for knowing so much. Or at least, for appearing to.

Tina blew another bubble.

'So what?' she said.

'So there's been rationing for ages. And now . . .'

'Now what?' said Tina.

'I don't know,' I said. 'But I know it's got worse, that's all.'

'So what?' said Tina, and I realised she didn't really want to know. She just wanted to get at me. She was still giving me a dirty look, as if the sight of me offended her.

I sighed. 'I suppose they'll fix it, anyway,' I said. 'Get everything back to normal. They always do.'

'Who's they?' said Tina.

She looked away and I took the opportunity to examine her a bit more closely. Her clothes were shoddy and worn, and she was thin enough to crawl through a letter-box. I realised that she inhabited a different world from me; a world without the supports that I had always taken for granted; without parents and schools and the comfort of cars. I couldn't imagine what that world would be like, but I had a suspicion that I might be about to find out.

Tina turned and caught me looking at her. I looked away. But after a minute she stepped closer and said, 'What's wrong with your brother?'

It would take too much effort to explain.

'He's not my brother,' I said.

Tina shrugged, and blew another bubble.

I bought myself some socks in Dunnes, and then coffees in Supermac's to bring with us to Stephen's Green. When we got there, we found a steady traffic of pedestrians going through, but it was too wet for people to be standing around, and we easily found a quiet corner. Darling had never got to eat her crusts, and she went off to where a scruffy old lady was feeding bread to a huge flock of pigeons. Despite perpetual squabbles, she did well enough for herself, darting in among the grey, feathery mass and snatching the best bits from under their noses.

When Oggy first spoke, my mind began to bend so hard that I was afraid it would snap. A bird was one thing; a step beyond mimicry. But a dog was something else. I brought all of the powers of my brain to bear upon it, but even the sharpest thinking was too blunt an instrument to carve comprehension out of the impossible, and I was left with only one option. To accept without understanding, that there were more things in the world than I had ever dreamt of.

As we drank the coffee I filled Tina in on what we were doing. She never looked at anyone who was talking to her, as though she was in a perpetual state of resentment against the whole world, but she was listening all right, and nothing escaped her. When Danny spoke she did a really cruel imitation of his sing-song speech. I found it deeply hurtful, but Danny just laughed, and after that he got on much better with Tina than I did.

'So if there aren't any buses, how do you propose to get to Dun Laoghaire?' She said it accusingly, as if it was a major planning error and I was directly responsible.

'You don't have to come,' I said, hopefully.

She ignored me. 'I can nick a car,' she said. 'If one of you can drive it.'

'I can,' said Danny. Luckily, Tina had the sense not to take him up on his offer.

nine

We walked the nine gruelling miles across the south side of the city, while the soft rain fell on our heads. We followed the bus route, but no buses came. And as the day wore on the traffic became thinner and the expressions on the faces of other pedestrians became more tense.

Trudging at Danny's slow pace was a lot more tiring than ordinary walking but, wet and miserable though I was, it was him I was worried about. I didn't know much about his history, but I knew that Maurice had always kept him quietly hidden at home. The furthest I had ever known him to go was the half mile to the woods and back. But, to my surprise, he turned out to have more stamina than either Tina or me, and he stayed cheerful and optimistic even when the rest of us lapsed into a tired, mechanical crawl.

It was well after dark by the time we arrived at the ferry port in Dun Laoghaire. The closer we got, the thicker the crowds became, and it was soon clear that Danny wasn't going to be able to manage the crush in the ticket hall. So we got him as near to the door as we could, and I persuaded him to sit down and rest for a while. The others stayed with him, while I joined the scrum and wriggled my way into the hall.

It was a lot worse than the bus station. Over the next fifteen minutes I learnt what it must feel like to be a sheep in a pen. After five minutes I gave up trying to make individual progress and allowed myself to be carried along, until eventually I came within sight of the ticket counters. They weren't even open. A big sign stood there instead.

TONIGHT'S SAILINGS FULL. PLEASE AWAIT ANNOUNCEMENTS REGARDING FURTHER SAILINGS.

I tried to resist the relief that began to infiltrate my mind. It would be embarrassing, of course, to have to back down, phone Maurice again, put up with the blame that would always be laid on me, no matter what I said. But he would come and get us, I was sure of that. Fuel or no fuel, he'd make it. Even if he had to push the car all the way here and all the way back. Maurice was like that.

And then I would be home; warm and dry, and free from the responsibility that was beginning to feel like a strain.

I set my face towards the door and waited for the next wave to carry me out. On the way I was jostled past a coffee stand and managed to hang on to it for long enough to put in an order. They had sold out of rolls and sandwiches, but they still had pre-packaged flapjacks and carrot cake slices, so I bought a dozen of each, and three large hot chocolates, and a bottle of spring water for Oggy.

It was quite an achievement to get it all out of there unspilled and unsquashed, but I succeeded. Danny was deflated when he heard about the tickets, but the grub was a feast and we all felt a bit better afterwards.

'Oh, well,' I said, pouring some of the bottled water into my empty cup for Oggy. 'That's the end of Scotland, I'm afraid. At least we tried.'

'I'm not going home,' said Danny. 'I'm going to Mother.'

'You'll have to swim, so,' I said.

'I will, then,' said Danny.

'You will not,' I said. 'You know you're terrified of anything deeper than the bath!'

'I'm not,' he said, stubbornly. 'I'm going to Mother. I'm going . . .'

He was struggling to get to his feet. I pushed him back down and he clobbered me so hard I saw stars.

'Hold your breath, Danny,' I said, trying to keep the desperation out of my voice. He was going to flip, I knew it.

'You hold it,' he said, pushing me aside and succeeding in getting up.

'Wait, wait, wait,' Oggy whispered, climbing between us like a referee and licking each of our faces in turn. 'I'll get us on the boat. Just hang around a bit, OK?'

Danny relaxed, as though entrusting his future to a sheepdog was quite natural. Oggy barked up at Darling in the rafters and the two of them vanished off into the darkness.

I squeezed into the warm spot beside Danny that Oggy had vacated.

'Easy for them,' said Tina, bitterly. 'Easy for a dog and a bird to sneak on to a boat. I bet they don't come back.'

'They'll come,' said Danny. 'They'll come.'

And they did, too. Sooner than any of us expected. Oggy jumped on to Tina's lap as if he was just pleased to see her, but I knew that he was saying something.

She looked surprised, and then scornful. 'Of course I can,' she said.

She stood up and gathered her things, gesturing to us to follow. Oggy led the way into the vehicle park, where the cars and vans that were going to make it on to the next sailing were standing in neat lines.

'Just act natural,' said Tina, as we made our way between them. I could see her reasoning; the area was well-lit and we couldn't have remained unseen no matter how hard we tried. But, a moment later, something happened that I should have been prepared for. And wasn't.

ten

Beyond the lines of waiting cars, beyond the looming bulk of the ferry, we got our first glimpse of the Irish Sea.

Danny froze, as though a sudden, unbearable pain had hit him between the eyes. Seeing him, I froze as well, stunned by my stupidity in having allowed this to happen.

Since Mom had married Maurice, I had never gone anywhere near the sea. It didn't bother me; I couldn't swim anyway and never saw the point in getting wet and cold. But Mom missed the water, and sometimes went off on her own for a walk or a swim at the coast.

Maurice said Danny had been traumatised by something that happened to him when he was a baby, and that the sight of the sea always made him flip his lid. He even turned off the television when those marine programmes came on, just in case Danny came in.

I ought to have remembered, somehow taken evasive action. But it was already too late. Danny was staring at the sea as though it was about to rise up and swallow him.

'Hang in there, Danny,' I said, standing in front of him,

blocking his view of the water. He shifted his gaze to me, and his expression was distant and inscrutable.

I grabbed at the chance. 'Let's go away,' I said. 'Away from the nasty water. Let's go home to Mom and Maurice and the nice, hot bath.'

It was the wrong tactic. I could almost see his resolve rise to the forefront of his mind.

'Scotland,' he said. With an effort of will, he averted his eyes and, as he followed after the others, kept his vision firmly fixed upon the ground.

At the edge of the waiting area a high wall separated the outgoing traffic from the incoming lanes and the customs sheds. Against that wall some of the last holiday makers of the year had parked their car and caravan, and a nice, dark pool of shadow lay behind them. As nonchalantly as we could, the five of us slipped into it.

Danny stood with his back to the sea while Tina worked at the lock on the caravan door. She was surprisingly quick and had just succeeded in getting it open when a man in a fluorescent yellow rain jacket appeared round the front of the car.

We were rumbled. My blood sang like feedback in my temples.

'Hello, lads,' said the man. 'This your car?'

He looked curiously at Danny's back.

'Yup,' said Tina, as casual as could be.

The man nodded. 'How many travelling?'

'Five,' said Tina.

The man nodded again, carefully counted out five flyers from a bundle under his arm and handed them to me.

'Special offer,' he said. 'Best stay with the car, now. We should be loading soon.'

We waited until he had gone out of sight, then climbed aboard the caravan. Tina and I were so relieved that it was hard to avoid falling around the place and giggling, but Danny lay down on the floor and stared at the ceiling, like someone in a trance. I could hear the waves lapping against the harbour wall.

'You sure about this, Danny?' I said.

He nodded, minimally.

'You have to be careful. You have to stay quiet and calm.'

Again he nodded and, as a sign that he understood, he took a deep breath and held it.

I let mine out and looked at the flyers by the weak light that leaked in between the curtains. They were vouchers, five pounds on each, to spend in the On Board Shop.

'Fat lot of use they are,' said Tina.

Then Oggy said, 'Shhh!'

We kept still and listened as a voice spoke over the tannoy.

'Will all passengers travelling by car on tonight's sailing please rejoin their vehicles now.'

As delicately as possible we all eased ourselves down on to the floor with Danny, where we lay in a damp, fuggy huddle, hardly daring to breathe. A few minutes later we heard the car doors open, one on each side, and slam closed again. After another few minutes the engine started and then, unbelievably, we were moving.

Despite my reluctance, my fear and my guilt, the spirit of adventure returned and filled my heart.

part three

one

As far as I could tell, Danny spent the whole journey staring at the ceiling, listening to the wash of the sea far beneath us. The gentle rolling of the ferry was comforting, womb-like, and the rest of us dozed; even Darling, perched on the edge of the caravan sink. It seemed like no time at all before the great engines ground and roared, and then died down as we docked.

I had been dreaming about talking sardines, and as I opened my eyes I could see why. Tina's foot was in my ear, Danny's head was on my shoulder, and Oggy was draped over my knee. But we were, at least, warm and dry.

'Now what?' I said, sitting up carefully and propping myself against the table leg. Tina yawned and tried to find room to shrug.

Around us now, we could hear the sounds of voices and slamming doors as the motorists returned to their cars.

'I dreamt I was comfortable,' said Tina. 'I dreamt I had a family.'

'Where is your family?' said Darling.

'I never had one,' said Tina. 'Not a proper one. The stork brought me to the wrong house. They hadn't ordered me at all.'

'Oh,' said Danny.

'Yeah, oh,' said Tina. 'Oh, oh. Double O.'

The car engine started up and the caravan began to inch forward along the deck.

'But what are we going to do?' I said. 'How are we going to get out?'

'Why do you want to get out?' said Tina. 'They'll have to stop some time, won't they?'

There was a metallic clatter as we came off the ramp, and then we were rolling along smooth tarmac.

'What if they get stopped at customs?' I said. 'What if they search the caravan?'

'What if the sky falls on our heads?' said Tina. 'We'll deal with it, that's what.'

There was a cupboard in front of her nose and she reached out and opened it.

'Oh, wow.' She pulled out a packet of Frosties, nearly full. 'My favourites, these.'

'You can't take them,' I said. 'They're not yours.'

But the packet was already open and Darling, who seemed to share Tina's opportunistic morals, dived in head first. Tina pulled her out and gave her a fistful on the draining board. Then she began to scoff them herself, and soon we were all at it, with Oggy hoovering up the dropped ones.

As the car moved through the town, the street lights were like strobes, brightening our little motor-home, then plunging it into darkness again. But before long we were sailing along the open road through the darkness.

'Where do you suppose we're heading?' I asked.

Tina shrugged. Danny said, 'Scotland.'

'Not north,' said Darling. 'More like southeast.'

'You'd know, I suppose,' said Tina.

'Yes. I would, actually,' said Darling.

'Got a compass in your head, then, have you?' said Tina.

'As a matter of fact I have,' said Darling. 'It's because I'm a bird. Whereas you, a human being, only have a faulty calculator in there.'

Tina took a swipe at her, but Darling flitted nimbly aside. She landed on Danny's head and began to comb his hair with her beak.

'How did you two learn to speak, anyway?' I asked Oggy.

'Mother taught us,' he said.

'Clever Mother,' said Danny, giggling, back to himself again now that the sea was far behind.

'And Father,' said Darling, 'And Sprog, and Colin.'

'Who's Father?' I asked. 'Who are Sprog and Colin?'

'Family,' said Oggy.

'Everyone talks at Fourth World,' said Darling.

'Fourth World?' I said.

'Our world,' said Darling. 'The world that Mother created.'

Instead of getting answers, I had been presented with more questions. I was going to ask them, but at that moment the engine of the car began to chunter and cough. The caravan lurched dramatically a few times and then, more smoothly, came to a stop. The car's tail-lights were still on, but otherwise the caravan was engulfed in darkness. For a long time we waited, and the only sound was the rain falling on to the thin roof.

'Let's make a run for it,' I said. But I had left it too late. A car door slammed and we could hear the clack of hard heels on the road. Then the other door slammed as well.

'But what if someone comes along?' said a man's voice.

The woman who replied was on the other side of the window, so close to us that her voice made us all jump.

'Oh, yeah?' she said. 'Like who? Good Samaritans in petrol tankers?'

She moved towards the door, and we could hear her fiddling with keys. 'I told you we should have stayed in Holyhead,' she grumbled. 'You never listen. You always know best.'

There was more key jangling, and then we watched the beam of a torch bounce past the window as the man joined her.

'Nag, nag, nag,' he said.

It was terrifying, sitting there in the dark waiting to be

discovered. I clutched at the flimsy little table, ready for anything. Danny's breathing was so loud and harsh that I was certain the couple must be able to hear it. I wanted to say something to calm him, but I didn't even dare whisper. The torch-light wavered about on the other side of the thin curtains, and weird shadows bloomed and swung. Then the key turned in the lock and the door opened.

Darling shot out like a black shuttlecock. The man ducked and for an instant the darkness was total again.

'What was that?' he said.

And then we were blinded by the beam. One by one we clambered out of the rocking caravan. Danny came last, all at sixes and sevens with himself. No one said a word until we were all out on the road, and then the man gathered his wits.

'What on God's earth do you think you're doing?' he said.

'Thanks for the lift,' said Tina.

'Lift?' said the man. 'We'll have to see what the police think about that.'

My heart missed a beat, but Tina was as cool as ice.

'Police?' she said, peering with exaggerated care into the empty darkness all around. 'Let's ask them, so, shall we?'

I started laughing, then. I couldn't help it. Danny joined in, and Oggy whined in sympathy.

'Get out of here,' said the man. 'If I see you again, I'll . . . I'll . . .'

75

'Yeah, yeah,' said Tina. 'I wouldn't get back in that tin can if you paid me.'

She set off into the night and we followed. Behind us the caravan door clicked shut, and when I looked back the torch-light behind the red curtains created a warm glow. They wouldn't have had to pay me to get back into it; not when I looked ahead of us at the alternative.

The road we were on was as black as sump oil. On either side the mountains reared up steeply and the night sky above them was only marginally paler. The rain wasn't heavy, but it had a persistent quality that was very familiar to anyone from the West of Ireland. As we rounded the first bend, and then the next, it became apparent that we were nowhere near any kind of civilization. Not a single light, near or distant, broke the blackness. There was no way of knowing how far we might have to go to reach shelter.

Oggy came to the rescue again.

'Hang about,' he said, and trotted off into the dark.

We dripped and waited. Darling went to sleep in my pocket, a warm little extra heart beside my own. Danny tried to scare us with ghost noises, but we were too wet and cold to be bothered. Oggy seemed to be gone for hours, but in reality it couldn't have been more than a few minutes before he reappeared.

'It's not great, but it'll do,' he said.

We followed him down the road for a hundred yards or so, then clambered over a loose stone wall and across the slippery hillside to where a huge, jagged rock jutted out of the sheer mountain wall and created an overhang. Beneath it, the ground was stony but dry.

It smelt of sheep, and we quarrelled about the best way to share the two blankets, but eventually we settled ourselves in. I turfed Darling out of my pocket and tried to get comfortable.

Tina was accustomed to living rough and went out like a light. Danny was his usual, contented self and, for once in his life, he was tired, since he hadn't slept. I was glad to see that he didn't need a sedative. If anyone did, it was me.

No matter how hard I tried, I couldn't sleep. I lay on the stony ground, feeling alone in my wakefulness, abandoned by the others. Around me the night was vast and eerily quiet. Behind the friendly sheep smell were wilder ones; of rain and rock and cold, cold earth. Above me, the sky went on for ever. Lost in its enormity, I drifted and dozed, and dreamt of infinite space, and loneliness, and the mournful calls of whales across the oceans of the earth.

two

Last to sleep and last to wake, I was pulled back from my dreams by someone rummaging in my pockets. I punched out with my elbow, and Tina squealed and called me something unrepeatable.

'Have you eaten them all, or what?' she said.

I sat up. Weak sunlight was leaking between two distant peaks and lighting our valley. Danny was awake, still wrapped in his blanket, and Oggy was below us on the hillside, patrolling. All my bones creaked with cold and damp as I sat myself up.

'Well?' said Tina, accusingly.

'Of course I haven't eaten them,' I said, digging into my pockets and bringing out what was left of the flapjacks and carrot cake. It was all pretty squidged up and some of the packages had burst, but we were hungry enough not to mind too much, and Darling disposed of the grittiest bits.

'I've got a grinder in there,' she explained, pointing a claw at her croup.

I noticed that she wasn't as all over black as I had

thought. The morning sunlight caught spangles of iridescence on her feathers, surprisingly beautiful against the grey-green landscape.

I kept back a flapjack for Oggy, who wolfed it down with a disappointing lack of appreciation.

'Now what?' I said. 'Are we going to hang around here all day?'

'Darling's gone to find a shop,' said Tina. 'So we can buy a map.'

Right on cue, she arrived back.

'There's a village about two miles east,' she said. 'I'll show you the way.'

Like *Cuchullain's sliotar* she bounced ahead of us, waiting for us to catch up before sailing off to the next perch. We dawdled along at Danny's pace, except for Oggy, who quartered the rocky slopes on both sides of us, his nose telling him things we couldn't begin to imagine. He put up a few rabbits, but he never came close to catching one.

'I could if I wanted to,' he told us. 'I'm saving my teeth for the big stuff.'

'Yeah,' said Darling. 'Those old horses in the Buddy tins.'

Tina and I laughed. But we were to learn, later on, that Oggy wasn't joking.

A few cars passed us, but not many, and none of them responded to Tina's hopeful thumb. We seemed to be walking for ever; more like four miles than two, but we got there at last. The village had a long main street lined with tourist shops and cafés, most of them closed for the winter season. There was a little filling station with a big sign which read; NO PETROL. REGULAR CUSTOMERS ONLY. Beside it was the mini supermarket that Darling had seen.

There were signs there as well, posted on to the door. NO BREAD. NO MILK. They didn't seem to be putting anybody off, though. The shop was full of people loading wire baskets with tins and packages.

We shopped fairly randomly, picking up anything we fancied that didn't need to be cooked. Oggy stood up and put his paws on my chest.

'Buddy, Christie,' he whispered, 'I like Buddy best. Loads of tins. Loads and loads!'

I put six tins into the basket, then biscuits, cheese, chocolate, bananas, apples. In the other aisle, Tina was loading Spam and condensed milk and tuna fish, and something of a feminine nature that I decided not to ask about.

Danny was standing at the check-out, frightening the cashier.

'Scotland,' he was saying, all full of glee and chuckles. 'We're going to Scotland.'

'What does he want?' the girl said, to no one in particular.

A man with a look of authority came in from the back of the shop and I dashed to the rescue.

'He wants a map,' I said.

'A map?' said the man. 'What does he want a map for?'

'We all want a map,' said Tina, hugging her loaded basket. 'Have you got any?'

He pointed to a rack beside the door, where maps and postcards were jumbled together. Then he turned to the woman behind Danny in the line. 'You can't take all those tins of powdered milk, Mrs Jones. We have other customers, you know.'

Like a light going on in my head, I realised what was happening. There was no bread and no milk because there was no petrol for the delivery vans, and now people were beginning to panic and stock up. A scary feeling began to creep under my skin and I glanced around at the stacked produce. Once it was gone, how would it be replaced? I remembered a picture on television of a Russian supermarket, all its freezers empty, all its shelves bare. Surely it couldn't happen here?

I wanted to get another basket; to grab anything and everything that might ward off the spectre of coming hunger. But it was too late. Mrs Jones was moving off, leaving a stack of powdered milk as a testimony to her fear. My own provisions were already being rung up, and Tina was adding her things to the basket as the cashier made room. I wiped the cold sweat from my forehead.

They would sort it out. Everything would soon be back to normal.

three

We went back out on to the road, lugging our plastic bags full of provisions and hitching, quite uselessly, the few cars and lorries that passed. Danny shuffled along, heroically but slowly, and our progress was minimal. I was already beginning to despair of ever reaching Scotland, but a couple of miles outside the village, to our surprise, we found a transport café with all its lights on. It had bright signs on the window, saying TIME TO FILL UP? and TRUCK IN AND TUCK IN, but inside it looked like a dingy and forlorn kind of place.

Danny and Tina went in, but Oggy was still whining about his Buddy, so I took him to the edge of the big lorry park to feed him. He wanted all the tins in one go. He nagged and nagged; said that he was starving and that it would save me having to carry it, so I compromised and tugged the ring-pull lids off three tins. He ate quicker than I could empty them, and then, as soon as he had finished the last bite, he went over the wall and threw up noisily. After that he was a bit more subdued, and agreed to wait outside the café for us.

For once, there was no shortage of anything. The only thing the café didn't have was customers. It must have catered for a fairly heavy traffic most of the time, and in the empty quiet of the place we could hear big freezers chugging away in the kitchens. The waitress was young and clearly bored witless. While our food was being cooked, she sat on a chair at the next table and leant over the back of it.

'Where are you headed?' she asked. We told her, and she squeaked with excitement, as though she could think of nothing more wonderful than a mid-winter trek into the unknown. When our meals arrived, she put loud music on the big juke box, but it only made the place seem even emptier and sadder than it was.

Tina and I finished long before Danny. We were dividing the shopping between our bags when we heard a truck pull in outside.

It was a bit like one of those psycho movies where the impossible suddenly starts to happen. Everything went still. Danny froze with his fork halfway to his mouth. Tina and I turned in our chairs. The chef and the waitress appeared in the doorway to the kitchen and stared. Then there were footsteps on the gravel, and a short, fat, bald man swung in through the door.

It was a bit of a disappointment, to be honest. The Lone Trucker ought to have been lean and swarthy; a worthy hero. I forgot about him and turned back to my packing, but Danny was still watching like a hawk.

'Mitch!' said the waitress. 'You must be the last driver on the road!'

'Ah, it's not that bad,' said Mitch. 'There are still a few things moving.'

'Where are you headed?' said the girl.

'Home,' said Mitch. 'I'm going to unhitch the trailer here if it's all the same to you. The cab should get me to Preston without it.'

Tina had put down her teacup and started rummaging for something in her bag. She sat back up again with the map in her hand, and nonchalantly spread it out on the table in front of us. We all leant over it. Behind us, Mitch ordered the *Eighteen Wheel Deal*. I could feel his eyes on our backs as we pored over the map. I was amazed by how long Scotland was and how far away from Wales. Somehow I'd had an idea that they shared a border, and that we just had to nip across and we'd be there. I wished I had listened in school.

'What bit of Scotland are we going to?' I asked Danny. 'Do you know?'

Danny grinned and pointed. I followed his finger up, and up, and up. It slowed and wavered somewhere around Inverness, as though it wasn't sure where to go next.

'But that's . . .' I became aware of Mitch again and dropped my voice to a whisper. 'That's a million miles! We'll never get that far!'

'We will,' said Danny.

Tina might as well have been deaf. She had located Preston on the map and was pointing at it. I focused in. It was right, bang on our route.

If we were going to Scotland.

Tina slipped away from us and over to Mitch.

'Will you bring us to Preston?'

'Get lost,' said Mitch.

'Please, Mister,' said Tina. 'We'll do anything.'

'We'll pay,' I said, carefully.

'Will you?' said Mitch. 'What'll you pay?'

'How much do you want?' said Tina.

The waitress arrived with a pot of tea and put it on Mitch's table.

'Go on, take them,' she said. 'They're from Ireland.'

'I can hear that,' said Mitch. 'What do they want to go to Preston for?'

'We don't,' said Tina. 'We want to go to Scotland.'

'Scotland!' said Mitch. 'You must be stark, raving bonkers.'

'Bring us, Mister,' said Tina, and then she put on a gruesome little girl face and said, 'Please?'

Mitch sighed hugely. 'Where's my flaming dinner?' he said.

four

He was a really good sort, that Mitch. I wished the world was full of him. He didn't bat an eyelid when he discovered that we had a dog, and with a bear's strength, he manhandled Danny up over the huge wheel-arch and into the cab.

'What happened to you?' he asked him, as he started the great engine and swung out on to the road.

'I had an accident,' said Danny, grinning broadly.

'What kind of an accident?' said Mitch.

'I don't remember,' said Danny.

'He was born like that,' I said.

Mitch nodded and turned his attention to his driving. The roads were practically empty and the cab, free of the weight it was designed to pull, hurtled along. Tina stared out at the passing scenery and Oggy slept at her feet.

'Do you think the petrol will come back soon?' I asked Mitch.

'It might and it mightn't,' he said.

The big engine wheezed and coughed as we eased up for a bend, then roared off hungrily along the straight.

'Are you worried about it?' I asked.

Mitch shrugged. 'Me, I take what comes. Even three kids and a dog.'

A Land Rover passed in the opposite direction and, a few minutes later, an old banger. Then it started to rain and, mesmerised by the wind-screen wipers, I dropped off to sleep.

I dreamt about a vast, empty factory with puddles of rusty water dripping from dead machines. The puddles were joining up and becoming pools, and then the water level was rising and I climbed up the walls into the giant steel girders of the roof, where a thousand black birds were squawking and flapping. Beneath me, Mom and Maurice were floundering in the flood.

We would never have got on to a train without Mitch. I think he must have known that, because he refused to drop us outside the station and leave us there. Instead he parked the truck and came in with us. The place was like a refugee camp, with people sitting and lying all over the floor. Restless travellers milled around above them, their faces angry or anxious, or simply bewildered.

For Danny the crowds were dangerous. For Tina and me they were suffocating, but Darling was safe among the pigeons in the high roof, and Oggy was in his element, introducing himself to anyone on the floor with licks and kisses, and relieving them of any bits of food that were not safely hidden. I was afraid that he'd make himself sick again, but Tina was terrified of losing him and wouldn't relax until Mitch gave up his belt as a lead. Oggy was deeply offended but Tina would not relent. As for Mitch, he was left with only one arm to battle with, since the other was needed for holding up his trousers.

But the inconvenience didn't stop him. He seemed to

delight in the challenge and, leaving us to fight our own corner, he ploughed a furrow through the congested lobby and disappeared. The rest of us found a few square inches of floor and staked it with Tina's blanket. We shared a packet of lemon cream biscuits, and Danny started singing his stupid football song again, but this time I didn't try to stop him. The whole place was bedlam anyway, and if it kept Danny quiet and happy, I could tolerate the odd looks we got.

In the end, Mitch was gone for more than forty minutes. I had begun to wonder if he had given up and gone home when he returned again, beaming with pleasure. He had four tickets; a full fare for Danny and half fares for me, Oggy and Tina.

'I spun them a yarn,' he said, proudly. 'I told them Danny needed to get to Inverness for urgent medical treatment.'

We all whooped with delight, but the rest of the news wasn't so good.

'Only as far as Glasgow, I'm afraid. They say they can't guarantee trains beyond that. You'll have to see what the story is when you get there.'

That dampened my spirits a bit, but not Danny's. He gave Mitch a clumsy great bear hug, and Oggy got all gooey and jealous and tried to join in. Mitch was like a beetroot on legs by the time he disentangled himself, but the colour soon faded. His face was grave and his tone was apologetic as he told us he had to go home.

'You couldn't have done more for us,' I found myself saying. 'We'll never forget you.'

Mitch nodded, and I thought his eyes got watery. But he turned away quickly and began to push his way through the crowds, and then he was gone. Out of our lives for ever.

part
four

one

By slow degrees we made our way to the Glasgow platform, and waited.

And waited.

When the train finally arrived, an hour and a half
late, we discovered that getting a ticket was only half
the battle. Now we had to get on. Every carriage was
packed to capacity, and the waiting passengers fought
so hard to get on that no one was able to get off. The
result was dangerous. Uniformed guards shouted instructions and struggled for order, but the crowds were
so dense and so desperate that they were overwhelmed.

Above our heads, Darling fluttered anxiously, waiting to
dart in with us if we looked like getting aboard. But we
found ourselves squashed so tightly that we couldn't
breathe, and I could see that Danny wasn't going to survive
for long in those conditions. By mutual agreement we
threw in the towel and squeezed our way back out of
the crush. We were rewarded with an empty bench which,

although we wouldn't have guessed it, was to become our home for the next few hours.

We weren't the only ones who failed to get aboard. When the train finally groaned its way out of the station, the exhausted guards found themselves the brunt of every-one's frustration, and I couldn't blame them for coming up with some snide responses. One of them dropped on to the end of our bench and wiped his brow with a striped handkerchief.

'None of this was in my contract,' he said, disregarding the NO SMOKING sign above the bench and reaching for a cigarette. He offered the packet to us, and Tina took one. While he lit up, Oggy began to sniff at his jacket pockets.

'Would you look at that?' said the guard. 'Got a sweet tooth, have you, boy?'

He produced a bar of chocolate and broke a piece off for Oggy, who took it with uncharacteristic politeness and swallowed it whole. Then he gazed up at his new friend with eyes full of gratitude and admiration.

The guard rubbed his head and scratched him behind the ears.

'I swear they're the most intelligent animals,' he said. 'We have an Alsatian at home and she understands every word I say. Every word. I bet this lad would talk to you if he knew how.'

Oggy gave me a look and I tried not to laugh.

'He would,' said Tina, dragging in cigarette smoke like a

surfacing diver. 'But he's going mental, missing our mother.'

Oh, they were a good team, those two. The affinity that existed between them was no coincidence. They already had the guard eating out their hands.

'You stick by me when the next train comes in,' he said. 'I'll get you on to it.'

But the next train didn't come in, nor did the one after that, and the waiting crowds thickened. From time to time a woman made an announcement over the tannoy, but her accent was so broad and the equipment so crackly that we gave up trying to understand what she said.

The day dragged on and we broke into our provisions again. Tina and I had a row over what we should eat first, and Oggy stole a packet of biscuits and scoffed them all under the bench before we noticed they were missing. I roared at him, Tina went into a huff, and up in the rafters the pigeons began ganging up on Darling. I began to wonder if there wasn't something catching in the air, like viral aggression or chronic infectious frustration. Luckily, Danny discovered his own way of dealing with the tension. He played trains up and down the platform, pretending to be an engine, chuffing and hooting, stopping beside other groups of passengers and inviting them aboard. It was embarrassing to say the least, but it was better than the trouble that would have ensued if I had tried to stop him.

At least our friendly guard seemed to be immune to the crazy atmosphere. He came back to tell us he hadn't forgotten us, and then went off again, promising to come back as soon as he had news of a train. After that, Danny got tired of being an engine, and he and Oggy went to sleep. Tina was still not talking to me, and I dropped into a well of loneliness.

Compared to all this, home seemed like heaven. Even Maurice didn't seem so bad, from this perspective. My loneliness brought me to a place within myself that I had never been willing to go to before, and for the first time, I realised that he had tried to be a good father to me. He had done things that my real father, estranged from my mother for most of my life, had never done. He offered to take me to hurling matches. I refused. He took an interest in the computer games I played, and offered to have competitions with me. I ignored him. He brought home the latest videos, which I declined to watch, even though I was dying to see them.

Why?

I knew why, now that I allowed myself to think about it. He had taken some of my mother's attention; that attention that had been mine and mine alone for as long as I could remember. And like a spoilt brat, I had been unwilling to share it. It wasn't Maurice's fault that I hated him. It was mine.

And he was right to be worried about Danny. He was

devoted to him; had been for all of his troubled life. A lot of people would have been glad to get rid of him; sent him to an institution or home to his mother. But Maurice took it all on, and did his stolid, patient best.

He would be going out of his mind with worry. So would Mom.

I huddled up against Danny on the bench and tried to sleep; to put it all out of my mind. But it wasn't going to happen. I had to let them know that we were OK.

I didn't know what I was going to say when I bought a phonecard from a vending machine and joined the queue for the booths. When I eventually got to the phone, the earpiece was warm and greasy from day-long occupation. It made me feel queasy, but I forgot about it the minute Maurice picked up. I still didn't know what I wanted to say.

'Christie? Where are you?'

'We're OK, Maurice. We're safe.'

'You're not. You're not safe. We want you here with us.'

It was as though his hand was reaching down the line and clutching at my heart. It was what I had been afraid of.

'Are you OK, Maurice?' I said. 'Is Mom OK?'

He continued as if he hadn't heard me. 'Listen to me, Christie. Don't hang up.'

'I won't,' I said.

'I'm going to put your mother on. Wait, will you?'

I waited, watching the numbers on the display window of the phone. £4.60. £4.40.

'Christie?'

I could barely talk past the lump in my throat. £4.20, read the display. £4.00.

'Hi, Mom.'

I knew now what I wanted to say. I wanted to go home. I wanted them to be here, now, with the warm car, waiting to take us all back to the safe, warm sitting room. I wanted to pig out and watch TV.

'Where are you?' said Mom.

'We're at the station . . .' I began. Then everything went haywire. The tannoy began to hiss and crackle, and I saw our benevolent guard weaseling through the crowds with surprising speed in the direction of our platform. I froze. Mom's voice said, 'What station, Christie?' but I didn't get as far as an answer. The guard had passed me and was vanishing down the stairs which led to our platform. There was no time to think. I couldn't let them go without me. I snatched the card from the slot, dropped the hand-set against the wall and ran out after the guard.

'Sorry, 'scuse me, sorry,' I said, barrelling through the crush and wriggling down the stairs towards the Glasgow platform. The train was already pulling in, and I would never have found the others if it hadn't been for Darling, who was hovering above their heads like a dark beacon. I held my breath and dropped my head and somehow tunnelled my way through the irate mob to where our guard, like a blue angel, was creating a one-man cordon around our little group.

They were just getting on the train. If it hadn't happened like that I might have tried to stop them; I might have talked to Danny and dissuaded him from going any further. But it was join them or lose them, and I wasn't about to get left behind on my own. I ducked under the guard's arm and he shoved me aboard. Above my head, Darling dived in with a whirring of wings, hovered frantically for an instant, then vanished ahead of us into the jam-packed carriage.

I didn't have time to worry about her. I was crammed against the toilet door and I could hardly breathe. Beside my knee I could feel Oggy squirming as he tried to avoid being trampled underfoot. A little further in, Danny was gaping like a squashed fish and Tina was valiantly trying to create some space around him.

There was a final, bone-crushing heave of flesh from behind, and the door closed. I looked back, hoping to see the guard and thank him, but all I could see was the nickel buttons on my neighbour's denim jacket. There were shouts and roars from the ones left behind but finally, unbelievably, the train began to move.

As I stood there, crammed against the door, I wondered why anyone had gone to the trouble of buying tickets. There was no way in the world that anyone was going to be moving along this train to check them.

three

As the train picked up speed, the people in the interior of the carriage relaxed their resistance and the pressure eased up. Someone fought their way through to the toilet and I was jostled away from the door. We manoeuvred our way across to the opposite side of the corridor and settled Danny down on a pile of luggage. As soon as he was happy again, playing spiders on the walls with his fingers, I went in search of Darling. To my relief, she was quite safe; sitting on a suitcase in the dark space between two seat-backs. She was probably better off there than she would have been in my pocket, so I left her where she was.

It was a nightmare journey. At every stop the angry scrummage was repeated, and if I was kicked and el-bowed and trodden on once, I was kicked and elbowed and trodden on a hundred times. Tina got quite savage about it after a while, and took to making faces at people and calling them names. It didn't create any more room for us, and it meant that we got excluded from the occasional air of camaraderie that wafted around the train, but there was no talking to Tina when she was in that kind of mood.

I turned away, as though I didn't know her. Danny's hands were still galloping around the walls and the stacked luggage. At least he was happy. But I wasn't. I was tired, and the home-sickness came back. For a while it overwhelmed me, and then I somehow passed through it, to where the bigger questions were lying in wait.

How had Maggie taught those animals to speak? What had she done to Danny, and what was she still doing that could give Maurice reason to report her? And who were these other characters that Darling had talked about? Father, and Sprog?

None of the questions had answers, not even in my imagination. It was easier in the end to turn them off and listen to the wheels clunking across the rail joints. Somewhere along the way the water ran out and the toilets began to emit a sickening stink. After that, I was so busy shutting things out of my awareness that I went off to sleep, upright and all as I was.

four

It was half-past four in the morning before the train finally reached Glasgow. The doors opened with a hydraulic sigh and an impossibly large amount of people spilt out on to the platform.

Darling was the last of us to emerge, and we regrouped on a bench, cold and befuddled.

'No more trains,' said Danny, and stood up, ready to move on.

'Wait,' I said. 'I want to stop and think for a minute. Have a discussion.'

'Ooh,' said Tina, sarcastically. 'A discussion, eh?'

I ignored her and blundered on. 'I just think maybe we've gone far enough.'

'Far enough for what?' said Tina.

'Just far enough. I want to go home.'

'Aah,' said Tina, with mock sympathy. 'Poor little poppet. Wants to go home.'

'It's all right for you,' I hissed. 'You're homeless anyway. I mean, if you're homeless you might as well be homeless here as there. It doesn't make any difference to you.' A soggy wave of self-pity rose into my nose and eyes. 'I have a home,' I said. 'I want to be in it.'

There was a pause, and then Tina said, 'All right. Now we've had our discussion. Let's have a vote. Who's for going home?'

I already knew I was outvoted, but I put up my hand anyway.

'And who's for going to Scotland?'

Tina put hers up. Danny pointed at the sky and whooped. Oggy howled like a Banshee, and Darling flew rings around and between us like a gigantic bluebottle.

My heart sank. As I trudged behind the others, out of the station and in to the dark city streets, I knew I was faced with two choices. One was to go along, whether I wanted to or not. The other was almost unthinkable. If I wanted to go home, to have my way, I would have to betray the others.

Outside the shelter of the station the wind was bitter. We pulled our coats around us and Tina released Oggy from the ignominy of Mitch's belt. He shook himself so hard his teeth rattled, then he romped like a puppy until Tina told him to act his age.

'Just warming up,' he said, sulkily.

With Darling navigating sleepily from my pocket, we set out across the city.

The power was down, and the streets were black with blacker shadows. Oggy tuned in to my anxiety.

'I'll protect you, Christie,' he said. 'No one tangles with Oggy.'

A man with a pale, slack face leant out precariously from a shop doorway.

'Did that dog just talk to you?' he asked. His voice was mumbly and I could smell the drink from three metres.

'You'd want to stay off that stuff,' said Tina.

*   *   *

By the time the sun began to lighten the sky we were passing through suburbs where dogs barked from behind closed doors and cats scowled at Oggy from high garden walls. And soon afterwards we found a little café, where we ate till we were full to the gills, and furtively slipped a few extra rounds of toast into our bags. When we headed out on to the road again, Danny seemed to be walking a bit faster and more smoothly than before. The rest of us still had to adjust our speed to his, but not as much. I found myself wondering why Maurice had always kept him so cooped up. Was it really for Danny's sake, or was it for some other reason? Because Maurice was ashamed of him, perhaps? It seemed to me as though this adventure was exactly the cure that Danny had been waiting for.

We were walking through an area of richer houses. Beyond them, a range of low hills rolled away into the distance. Oggy bounded ahead of us, exploring every garden and field and hedgerow along the way. The chill wind had dropped and the sun was making the hills glow with green promise. Darling ignored us all for a while, then took it upon herself to perform for us. She sat on a telegraph post and came out with the most amazing set of impersonations. She did a chicken first, then an alarm clock, then a curlew and a jackdaw and a sheep. And once she had our full attention, she got us all in stitches by mimicking All Saints, Marge Simpson, and Oggy begging for Buddy. For the moment, at least, I forgot that I didn't want to be there, and we covered the next few miles in companionable silence.

There was very little traffic on the road, but there was some. Whenever a car passed, Tina thumbed it with frenzied enthusiasm, but I was sure that she only made us look even weirder than we were, and she didn't have any success. We walked on and put slow miles behind us, and at around midday we stopped for a break and a bite to eat. We felt that we had gone for miles, and we were all in great spirits until Tina got out the map. Then we deflated. All those hours of walking did not even add up to one inch of progress. We were barely clear of Glasgow.

It put the journey ahead into cruel perspective. We had grown up, all of us, in a world where walking was a leisure activity and not a means of travel. A hundred miles to me meant boredom in the back of a car. But now that I had just barely covered six in an entire morning, the concept of distance changed in my mind, quite dramatically.

When we felt rested enough we set off again. As the afternoon wore on, the sky clouded over and mist engulfed the higher points of the hills. Darling floated above us like a guiding star, and the way ahead was constantly marked by the waving white flag of Oggy's tail. I remember a moment of perfect peace, when I felt as though I could have gone on for ever like that, strolling with my friends towards Inverness.

But afterwards I came to see that glowing moment as the

calm which comes before the storm. Because it was very soon afterwards that everything started to go wrong.

Another car came flying along the road, and as Tina stuck out her thumb I could see that she was sharing my mood. Her hitching performance, normally urgent and weird, was suddenly quite relaxed and charming. I had always thought of Tina as awkward looking; too thin and gawky to be pretty. But when she was happy and not hunched up over herself, she looked quite different; almost beautiful. There was a man in the car and as he approached us I could see his expression change as his attention shifted from the road and on to Tina. He slowed, and peered closely at her as he passed, then seemed to drift hesitantly for a hundred yards or so. Finally, to our amazement, he stopped.

Tina and I sprinted over the distance and Danny hobbled after us, not that far behind, with Oggy. The man got out of the car and waited for us on the passenger side. When we caught up to him he looked Tina up and down, then smiled at me.

'Going far?' he asked.

'Inverness,' I said.

'You're a long way from Inverness,' he said. Then his eye fell on Oggy.

'That your dog?'

I nodded.

'I'm not having a dog in my car,' he said. 'You'll have to leave him.'

I stepped away from him, and maybe some instinct was at work deep within me, because I remember feeling vaguely relieved.

'We can't leave him,' Tina was saying. She was laying on the charm again and it made me uneasy. 'He's very quiet, honest. You won't even know he's there.'

Danny had caught up at last and was already climbing into the back of the car. The man didn't pay him any attention at all.

'All right,' he said. 'If the dog goes in the boot I'll take you as far as I'm going. That's my final offer.' He opened the passenger door and Tina dropped her bag on the floor and got in. Then he came round and opened the boot.

There was plenty of room for a dog in there, but Oggy was behaving very strangely. He couldn't say what was on his mind, but he expressed himself pretty well all the same. He whined and put his tail between his legs and refused to come over when I called him. I thought he was just being sniffy about having to travel in the caboose, but the truth was that his instincts were far more highly attuned than ours were.

'Do you want us to go without you?' I said.

He whined and cringed and wagged his tail, but he wouldn't come. I was so sorry afterwards for what I did next, but at the time it seemed like the only thing to do. I threw my bags into the back of the car, grabbed Oggy by the scruff of the neck, and lifted him bodily into the boot.

The man slammed the lid and went round to the driver's side. As soon as his back was turned, Darling drifted down on silent wings and I picked her out of the air and slipped her into my pocket. I got into the back with Danny and, before long, we were a snoring jumble of heavy limbs.

I woke with a start.

'Out, lads,' the man was saying. 'Quick, now.'

I stared out with bleary eyes. It was pitch dark and the headlights were illuminating a junction where two roads met. The road we were on was steep at that point, and the man was holding the car on the clutch. Tina had her head down, getting her bag, I supposed.

'Come on,' he said. 'I'm turning right here and you need to go left. Out you get.'

Danny already had his door open and I fumbled at mine and spilt out, dragging my plastic bags behind me. I was already on the road when I heard Tina shout.

'Let go of me!'

She had opened her door and by the inside light I could see that the man had a tight grip on her arm and was preventing her from getting out. I dropped my bags and grabbed Tina's door, but the swine was already letting off the clutch and the car was pulling forward.

We were lucky that Darling had her wits about her. With the courage of a lion she flew at the man's face and went for his eyes with her beak and claws. I don't suppose he had any idea what was happening. He let out a yell and threw up his hands to protect himself, letting go of Tina in the process. I pulled her out and, luckily enough, her foot caught in the shoulder-strap of her bag and it got dragged out behind her, spilling its contents on to the road. Behind Tina, Darling left off the attack and swept out of the car just as it roared like a jet plane and careered away.

Danny was trembling and gasping. We all were. We watched the red tail-lights diminish and disappear, and then there was a full minute of shocked silence before Tina's heart-broken wail rent the night air.

'Oh no! Oh no! Oh no! Oggy!'

And then Danny flipped. It was too much, and for the first time on the journey he lost control. I saw him going.

'Hold, Danny. Hold your breath,' I said. But it was already too late. He was making terrible whooping sounds, dragging in huge lungfuls of air, and his eyes had that dreadful look that I knew so well: huge and wild and vacant.

Tina backed off, terrified. I did what I had seen Maurice do on a few occasions—I grabbed Danny and hugged him tight. But he was too far gone and he thrashed around so hard that I was in danger of getting hurt and had to let go. For a few more moments he gaped and gasped, lumbering around in the road and crashing against the hedges and walls. I was terrified that he was going to hurt himself, out here in the middle of nowhere, but he was so far gone that he didn't even hear my warnings. Three times he staggered and fell, three times he got up again and blundered about, like a blind, enraged monster. And then, finally, he dropped like a felled ox, out for the count.

I had seen it happen before, but Tina was terrified.

'Oh, Jaysus,' she said. 'Oh, Sweet Jaysus.'

I knelt over Danny and felt his pulse. It was rapid and strong.

'He's all right,' I said. 'He just goes over the top sometimes. He hyperventilates.'

'Hyper what?' said Tina.

'Too much oxygen,' I said. 'He'll sleep it off.'

Together we pulled him out of the road and on to the verge. I wrapped his blanket around him and made him as comfortable as I could.

'Now what?' said Tina.

'We just have to wait,' I said. 'We might as well try and get some sleep.'

'Sleep!' said Tina. 'Sleep!'

'Sleep,' said Darling, like a little echo. 'Sleep.'

She flitted up into a tree and fell silent. I lay down beside Danny and dragged a bit of the smelly blanket over my shoulders. A short distance away, I heard Tina settling herself in. I couldn't be sure, but I think she was crying.

part
five

one

In the morning Danny was fine. I could see Tina looking at him dubiously, but it was always the same. If he ever had any memory of his turns, or any bumps or bruises, he didn't mention them.

I had hoped that the man might remember Oggy and dump him out, but there was still no sign of him, and Darling's hopeful recce failed to find anything. We were all sad, but Tina was inconsolable.

'He was the best friend I ever had,' she moaned, hiding her face in the folds of her old, grey blanket.

'We're your best friends,' said Danny. He was concerned about Tina, but full of his usual delight, despite what had happened. At times like that, I sometimes felt that he was *more* than human, not less. What people could be, if the world was perfect. But his charm was lost on Tina.

'You don't count,' she spat, savagely. 'You're both going to turn into men!'

I wanted to protest, and Danny was totally confused by

the idea, but there was no denying it. I had never thought of myself in those terms, and wondered if it was something else I ought to feel guilty about.

'I would never do something like that,' I said.

'Nor would I,' said Danny, but Tina didn't seem convinced. She got up and began to walk away, and there was nothing Danny or I could do except follow.

Either the mist had dropped or we had been driven up into it during the night. We walked on through it, with Darling ahead of us, vanishing and emerging again, giving a strange, slow rhythm to our march. We had little idea of where we were going, except that we were still heading north, and the muffling mist made our senses all but redundant, and threw us back in on ourselves.

It was not a good time for that to happen. Tina was more remote than ever, and Danny got gimpy and slow again. As for me, I brooded. It wasn't fair that I had to be doing this. I was almost like a captive, forced along on this bizarre and dangerous journey against my will. By the time we stopped for lunch I was ready for a fight.

'It's all your fault,' I said, breaking up a bar of chocolate and, meanly, keeping the biggest piece for myself. 'How is it that your mother just happened to send for you just now, eh? When everything's going haywire?'

Danny sniggered. 'Haywire,' he said. 'That's funny.'

My blood began to boil.

'There's nothing funny about it!' I yelled. 'I don't want to be here, understand? I don't even know where we're supposed to be going!'

All three of them just stood and stared at me, as though I was the one who was mad, and not them. I stood up and began to walk back the way we had come. I suppose I thought the others would follow me, but they didn't. I kept going, unwilling to back down now that I had tried to make a stand, but I was getting scared, being out there on my own, and despite what Maurice had said, I felt responsible for Danny.

Besides, I had all the money. In the end I had to stop. But I wasn't ready to go back to them, yet. I wasn't going to back down that far.

I sat on a wobbly stone wall in the damp, misty afternoon, and waited. Eventually, Darling arrived. I knew she was there but I didn't look up. She tried to win me over by doing more impersonations; an owl, a football crowd, an opera singer, but I refused to be amused. Then she did a duck, and I couldn't help laughing.

'Come on, Christie,' she said. 'We need you.'

I shook my head. 'I just don't know what's going on,' I said. 'You've got to explain things to me, Darling.'

'Explain what?'

'How you and Oggy can talk, for one thing.'

But Darling just looked perplexed. 'I don't know, Christie,' she said. 'How did *you* learn to talk?'

119

'But that's different. All people can talk. But animals can't. They just can't.'

Darling hopped on to my arm and gobbled up a small spider that I hadn't noticed. 'All I know is that we're not supposed to tell anyone. Except you and Danny.'

'Why?'

Darling had to think hard about that one. Eventually she said, 'I think it's something to do with Mother's lab. She doesn't want anyone to know about it.'

'Her lab?'

Before Darling could reply, Danny and Tina emerged from the mist, and I remembered that I was sulking.

'Come on, Crimpy,' said Danny.

I looked away, remembering his mother. Striding down the street. A lab. So she really was a scientist. And maybe not so mad, if she had found a way of altering animal behaviour.

'We're going, whether you like it or not,' said Tina. 'Do you think we care if you come?'

'Thanks, Tina,' I said. 'I'm definitely not coming now.' Even though I wanted to again. More than ever. To see the lab, to know more about what Mother was doing.

'I care, Christie. I care,' said Danny. He was distressed, and beginning to wind up. I glared at Tina. She looked away.

'All right,' she snarled. 'I want you to come, OK?'

It wasn't the enthusiastic response I would have liked,

but it was enough to let me off the hook. Danny made delighted whooshing noises and threw his arms all over the place. Together again, we walked on into the enveloping mist.

two

As night fell, we came upon a little farmhouse and, with Darling on the look-out, succeeded in sneaking into a dry outhouse at the back of the yard. It was a fuel shed, with a big stack of musty logs in one corner and neat bundles of kindling in another. In a third corner was a stack of old cardboard boxes and newspapers and, with a bit of quiet labour, we spread them out and made a fairly level sort of bed. It wasn't much, but after the bone-deep dampness of the misty night it was five-star luxury. The covert adventure brought us all together again, despite our tiredness. We might even have been happy for a while, if it hadn't been for Oggy. His absence was even louder than his presence, and we missed him terribly.

We shared some more chocolate and were jostling for position under the blankets when we heard the farmhouse door click open. The window of the shed had no glass in it, and the sound seemed horribly close. Then a torch beam began to strobe across the darkness, a man coughed, and slow footsteps advanced towards our door.

Tina went rigid with fear. Danny's breath rasped like a saw, until I whispered to him to hold it. For once, he did. Above our heads, Darling dropped down from the rafters and drifted out through the window like a leaf on the breeze. The footsteps were closer, and we heard the soft creak of a log basket meeting the ground. There was no escape now, and we were all wondering what to do and say, when the shrill, urgent tones of a ringing phone began to sound.

The man swore and retraced his steps, more rapidly this time, back to the house. With our hearts in our mouths we jumped up and felt around for our gear in the darkness. The log basket went flying as we pelted out and across the yard to the gate and the public road beyond. Danny moved faster than I had ever seen him go; covering the ground in long, gallumphing strides. We didn't slow down until we were well clear of the farm and quite sure that no one was coming after us. As we were recovering our breath, Darling caught up with us.

'Phew! That was lucky,' said Tina.

'Call it luck if you like,' said Darling, clinging to the front of my jacket and trying to open the zip with her beak.

'What do you mean?' I said, opening it up and helping her into my pocket. She nestled down comfortably, then stuck out her head and performed the perfect telephone noise all over again.

three

Our exhilaration was short-lived. We walked through most of the night, along winding roads which seemed to have far more uphills than downhills. In the darkness our map was useless, and once again we found ourselves relying on Darling. I wondered how we would have managed without her.

To keep pace with Danny I fell into a meditative amble, like a monk taking a constitutional around his cloister. With our bodies on automatic and our minds on standby we trudged on through the darkness until eventually, just before dawn, we found some trees and a high wall leaning together like conspirators. In the inky shadows they created, we dropped to the ground and slept like the dead.

I was woken by a clamour of unruly voices. Above me the trees were black and fluttering, and for a moment I thought the world had gone mad. Then I realised that it was starlings, thick as foliage on the bare branches. A solitary rook perched among them, lonely as a teacher in a playground.

Darling was lost in the clamouring mass, just one among hundreds. 'Darling!' I called, and my urgency woke Tina. 'Darling!'

There was something vaguely wimpish about being so attached to a little bird, but I was still missing Mom and Maurice, and now Oggy, and I wasn't ready to lose someone else as well, no matter how small they might be. But she wasn't lost. She floated down from among the masses and landed on my blanket.

'Don't panic, Christie,' she said, picking small twigs and bits of leaf-mould out of my hair. 'I was just gathering a bit of information, that's all.'

Beside me, Danny woke up and stretched.

'Good riddance to that mist,' he said.

I hadn't noticed the obvious. Through the network of branches and between the circling starlings, the sun was shining bright.

We finally figured out how to use the tin opener on my penknife and, while we were eating, another flock of starlings came sweeping across the white sky like a swarm of bees. Their wings sounded like flitters of cloth in a breeze.

Darling bolted her share of tuna and vanished among them, making me anxious again. Their chatter was deafening, containing the most amazing variety of sounds, and I found that I could imagine how it contained information; a language based on the mimicry of what had been heard in the environment.

After a few minutes, Darling rejoined us.

'Bad weather ahead, they're all making for the south, there's snow in the mountains and more on the way.'

'How do they know?' said Tina, still yawning. 'Been watching the weather reports, have they?'

'They're birds,' said Darling. 'They know how to read the winds.'

'Just wondering,' said Tina.

The starlings lifted off with a ripping, raining sound like a sudden squall. For a moment the sky was dark with them as they banked and wheeled and made extraordinary patterns of themselves against the light. Then they were gone, and I could sense Darling's loneliness as she gazed after them into the empty sky.

'Some of them spotted a dog on his own,' she said at last. 'It might have been Oggy.'

'Where?' I said.

'Just somewhere,' said Darling, vaguely. 'Not here.'

'That's useful,' said Tina. 'Did your pals ever think of applying for a job with Interpol?'

Darling got into a huff and hopped off to pester the sad rook. The rest of us decided to do a stock-take and tipped everything out of our bags on to the ground.

There were some crazy things in Tina's bag; a big chunky

candle, some incense, a tiny brass bell. There were drabber things, too, battered and unrecognisable but clearly of value to her because she stowed them all away, quickly and possessively. She had a bent coat hanger in there as well, and that mysterious pink packet that she had bought in Wales.

'What do you need all that junk for?' I asked.

But Tina just glared at me, and suddenly I knew, and felt bad. Those pathetic bits and pieces were all she owned in the world.

The plastic bags were in flitters and we wrapped what was left in the blankets. There was disappointingly little. Two packets of home-wheat biscuits and one of cream crackers, two tins of Spam, one of peaches, and a big bag of peanuts. The only other food was Oggy's; the last two tins of Buddy.

'We can ditch that,' said Tina.

But I couldn't. Like her bits, they were things I had to carry. If I let go of them, I let go of Oggy. And I wasn't ready to do that, yet.

Despite the food situation we decided to bypass Stirling and steer due north. But as soon as we were out on the road again, Tina discovered that her shoes were falling apart. Danny and I both had good boots, but Tina's trainers were cheap rubbish and the soles had started to come away from the uppers. It must have happened during the previous night's monk-walk, when she was too detached to notice, but now it was clearly a serious problem.

We got out the map again and reconsidered.

'If it's shoes we want,' I said, 'we'll have to go to town.'

four

The supermarkets in Stirling were mobbed, and we didn't go near them. But the shoe shops were practically empty, and Tina chose a pair of leopard-spotted Doc's. She walked nine miles high in them, and stopped every ten metres or so to look down and check that they were still there. I was sure she had never had anything like them before, maybe nothing new at all, and I felt proud to have been able to provide them for her, even though the money hadn't exactly been mine.

Afterwards we bribed our way into a fancy hotel, and for an hour or so we inhabited a different world, eating with the finest silver spread endlessly on starched, white linen. But when the wafer-thin mints were gone, and we were back on the road, the stark reality of who we were returned. Just three young tramps, with a long, long road stretching out ahead of us.

five

Within a mile, Tina's new boots had raised big, watery blisters on her heels. It looked as though our run of good luck had ended, but it hadn't. We were sitting beside the road, examining Tina's feet and wondering what to do next when a flashy four-by-four pulled in beside us. A woman was driving, and she opened the window and stared at Tina's feet.

'Are you in trouble?' she said.

She turned off the engine and got out to examine the blisters.

'I might be able to help you, there,' she said, opening the rear door of the Jeep. The back was stacked high with medical supplies.

'Hazel Walker. Flying doctor,' she went on, with a grin. 'Where are you headed?'

I turned to Danny, realising with a chill that the best indication we had ever got was his wobbly finger, somewhere around Inverness. I wondered if he even knew. If he had heard the doctor's question, he gave no indication of it.

He was gazing at the surroundings, a beatific smile on his face, in some world of his own.

'What is the address, exactly?' I asked him.

He turned, looking puzzled.

'Mother's address?' I said, trying to sound casual, trying not to sound like a runaway. 'I've forgotten.'

Danny thought for a minute, then reached into the back pocket of his jeans. He pulled out a very crumpled piece of paper and handed it to me. On it was printed, in capital letters, MAGGIE TYLER, BETTYHILL, HIGHLAND.

'Bettyhill,' I said to the doctor.

'Bettyhill!' she squawked, her jaw dropping to her lap.

I tried to act nonchalant, but my heart was doing somersaults.

'You have some travel ahead of you, then,' she said. 'I'll take you as far as I'm going, but it won't knock much off a journey like that!'

A few minutes later, Tina was patched up and back in her precious boots, and we were all settling into the plush upholstery of the four-by-four. Hazel told us that she had just been into Stirling to collect supplies. She showed me a docket on the dash which exempted her from petrol rationing.

'I do a lot of home calls,' she said. 'And the odd bit of mountain rescue. Essential services.'

She was enchanted with Darling, and stroked her on the head with two fingers.

'Isn't he gorgeous?' she said. 'I had a pet jackdaw, once. He used to sit at the window and talk to me. Made all sorts of wonderful noises.'

'Darling makes great noises, too,' I said. 'Do a chicken, Darling. Buck buck. Buck buck.'

But Darling just stared at me with a bland, uncomprehending eye, and I zipped her quickly back into my jacket.

Mother had taught her well.

six

Hazel dropped us in Dalwhinnie, where she had a call to make. From the windows of the Jeep we got our first sight of the Cairngorms, looming above us to our right, their snowy peaks stretching up into the low clouds.

'Stick to the A9 all the way to Inverness,' she said. But she didn't let us go without adding a few things to our supplies. She gave us a huge tin of shortbread biscuits that a grateful patient had given her. In a resealable plastic bag she packed a first-aid kit, with dressings for Tina's blisters, a tube of antiseptic, some butterfly plasters, and a bandage. And as an afterthought, she dug out a foil space-blanket, and told us to use it if anyone got dangerously cold.

'Just in case,' she said. But none of us imagined how soon we would come to need it.

The afternoon was bright and clear, and we felt rested after the ride in the Jeep. The hedgerows were full of redwings feeding on haws and holly, and Darling flitted among them, noisy and belligerent.

A few cars passed us, and a tractor, and once, to our surprise, a bus. We flagged at it desperately, but it was stuffed to the gills, and the driver just shrugged, helplessly. As the afternoon wore on towards evening, dark clouds appeared in the northwest and gradually spread over the sky, evicting the sun. Soon after that, Darling returned from a scouting trip with snowflakes on her wings and, a moment later, the blizzard was upon us.

Tina squealed with excitement and my head filled up with the promise of snowball fights and sleigh-bells, but our glee didn't last for long. Darling demanded to be let into my pocket. The cold snow stung our eyes and made Danny gasp, which was dangerous.

'Take it easy, Danny,' I said. 'Try not to huff and puff, OK?'

He did his best. I suppose I thought the shower might just pass over, but before long we were isolated from our surroundings by a gliding grey dome of swirling flakes. In no time at all the road had gathered a coating of slippery white fluff, and it looked as though we were in for the long haul.

'Maybe we should go back?' I said.

Danny shook his head, determinedly.

I turned to Tina for support, but she just shrugged, infuriatingly.

'Don't you care? What if we get trapped in a blizzard and freeze to death?' I said.

She shook her head.

'Oh, come on!' I said. 'Danny doesn't know the difference. He thinks all this is a game.'

Danny laughed delightedly and began to try and gather the thin snow for a snowball.

'You see?' I said. But Tina just shrugged again. I could have throttled her.

'Right, so,' I said. 'We'll freeze to death. See if I care.'

I marched forward through the blizzard, not caring whether Danny could keep up or not. But after a while I couldn't see them when I looked back, so I slowed up and waited.

A car passed us, its driver leaning forward and peering out behind the rapid action of her windscreen wipers. Within five minutes, the same car came back again, and this time the driver shook her head at us and gave us the thumbs down.

But still we pushed on, past the tyre-marks where the car had turned, and on beyond them, into the storm. Before long we were leaving deep imprints and the trees and hedges beside the road were gathering tiny drifts on their leaves and branches. It was beautiful, I suppose, but it was a sinister, dangerous beauty, and I could not enjoy it. We passed the gateway to a house, and a whiff of smoke reached us with its promise of warmth and safety. I remember a fleeting thought: this is our last chance. But we didn't stop. We bent our heads against the blinding snow, and fell into a steady, plodding rhythm, and around us the last of the daylight began to fade.

It was almost dark when we came upon the abandoned car. It was covered in snow; blank and round as an igloo, but it was the best we were likely to find. We scraped the doors clear and Tina worked her coat hanger magic, then we all clambered in and hunched up together in the back.

It was cold, but the wind couldn't get at us and it was better than being outside. The inside light was working, and Danny started a game of *I Spy*, which, since he couldn't read or spell, was hilarious. Soon the whole car was shaking with our laughter. It entertained us for ages, and when we finally got bored of it we were all tired enough to curl up and go to sleep.

It was a miserable night. Cramped and cold, we dozed in fits and starts, but nobody really slept. In the early hours I woke so cold that I unpacked the foil blanket and spread it out over the three of us.

My flounderings in the cramped space disturbed Darling from her roost on the headrest, and she made a raucous, scolding sound. I tried to sleep again, but I was still cold.

'Darling?' I said.

'What?'

'Who is Father?'

She didn't answer.

'And who is Sprog?' I went on.

'Don't call her Sprog. She doesn't like it.'

'You did.'

Darling chuckled in the darkness. 'Not supposed to.'

'But who is she? And who is the other one? Colin?'

'Not like us,' said Darling. 'Not like you. Danny's brother and sister.'

'What?' I said.

Abruptly, Tina thrust her elbow into my ribs.

'Ow!'

'Will you shut up, the pair of you,' she snapped. 'Some of us are trying to sleep!'

The space-blanket seemed too light to make any difference, but I noticed that I was already warmer. And the next thing I knew, daylight was leaking around the edges of the drifts which had banked up against the car.

seven

The air was fuggy and stale in the car, and I had a headache, but Danny was calm and clear-headed.

'How far have we got to go?' he asked.

I rolled down a window and a little drift of snow fell in on top of us. We got out the map and eventually found Bettyhill, right up on the northern coast.

'Oh, God,' I said. 'It's a million miles away. We'll never get there.'

'We will,' said Danny. 'I know we will.'

'Why are we doing this?' I asked. 'Does anybody know?'

'We're going to find Mother,' said Danny.

'I know that,' I snapped. 'But why? Why can't we just go home and get on with our lives?'

'Because we're going to find Mother,' said Danny.

I wasn't getting anywhere, and with a hollow feeling inside, I gave up again.

We ate biscuits and peanuts, then wrestled our way out of the drifted-up car. The blizzard had died down, and the fallen snow was clean and smooth, exciting in its untouched vastness. We snowballed our way along the empty A9, until Tina knocked Darling out of the sky with a direct hit and gave us all a fright. She was all right, but after that, we conserved our energy for walking.

I fell in beside the others.

'Have you got a sister?' I asked Danny. 'And a brother?'

Danny laughed, and put a heavy, bear-like arm around Tina and me. 'Brother and sister,' he said.

The going wasn't too heavy, and our progress was good, so good that I allowed my hopes to rise. We might even make Aviemore by nightfall, and if not, we were sure to find somewhere to sleep. To our left, the huge cliffs of the Monadhliath mountains loomed over us, but there were houses and farms at the feet of the Cairngorms on the other side, and it seemed a safe enough kind of area. But things didn't work out as I had hoped. Soon after we had stopped for lunch a new storm closed in, leaving us as blind as before and, if anything, colder.

I don't know how or when we left the A9. All I know is that at some stage during the late afternoon it suddenly became clear that the road we were following wasn't it. The A9 was a main trunk road and had a certain dignity about it, but this road didn't seem to know what it was up to. It jinked and turned in all sorts of directions; sometimes broad, sometimes narrow. The only thing it seemed to be consistent about was its incline. We hadn't intended it, but we were climbing steadily into the mountains, and night was approaching fast.

'There have to be houses,' said Tina, expressing the fear that we had all begun to feel. 'They don't build roads into nowhere.'

But it felt like nowhere, and I was fast losing confidence in *They*. We couldn't see much in the daylight. When darkness closed in, we could see nothing. We could have passed within feet of a barn or a cottage without knowing it was there. The blizzard showed no sign of relenting; if anything the snow was falling more heavily than ever. Although I couldn't see them, I was acutely aware of the presence of those craggy peaks, standing over us like malevolent gods, indifferent to our puny sufferings. A guy who had climbed Everest had come to talk to our school, once. Our teacher introduced him by saying that he had conquered the highest mountain on earth, but he had shaken his head. He said that nobody conquers mountains; the luckiest climbers survived them, that was all. He told us how quickly a person can die in the snow, and now I wished that he hadn't.

Since we could no longer see, we progressed by feeling our way, zig-zagging between roadside walls and hedges. We struggled on, until even the road seemed to have disappeared, and I was sure that I could feel grass and stones beneath the snow instead of tarmac. Danny was finding the going difficult, and I could hear danger signs in his breathing; a little whimper of anxiety now and then, or a fearful gasp.

'Don't be worrying, Danny,' I said. 'We'll find somewhere soon.'

'Yeah,' he said. 'Somewhere soon.' I was touched by his confidence in me. I wished I could persuade myself so easily.

I prayed for a house, a shed, a cave; anything, but if there was anybody there, he wasn't answering. In the end we settled for the best we could get; a sheer wall of rock which loomed out of nowhere and stretched into the nothingness above our heads.

It wasn't snow-proof, but it was wind-proof. I let Darling out of my pocket while Tina and I cleared a space in the drifts big enough for us all to camp down. For all her sarcasm and attitude problems, Tina was brilliant in a crisis. We worked together as if we were telepathic, and no one had to be the boss and tell anyone else what to do. I realised that I liked her, despite her annoying manner, and I wondered how long it was since I hadn't. I couldn't remember changing my mind. I wished she would like me.

By the time we had finished digging, I was feeling OK, but Danny was in a bad way. He was talking nonsense and wanted to keep walking, so we had to drag him off his feet and lower him down into our little bivouac. With freezing fingers I unpacked the space-blanket again, and Tina helped me to wrap Danny up in it like a Christmas turkey.

141

Then we settled down, one on each side of him, and pulled the two blankets over us all.

It was only then that I remembered Darling. I called out to her in the darkness, but she didn't answer and she didn't come. Frantic, I got up and searched with numb hands across the rocks and snow. I couldn't bear to lose her; I just couldn't bear it. But I couldn't find her, either, and eventually, snuffling with hot tears, I returned to my icy bed.

eight

I don't know whether I slept and dreamt, or whether Death kept me awake while it showed me its works. I don't remember half that I saw, but the visions were clearer than day and vast as the sky.

I lay on a battlefield watching my blood drain away, and I sank down through fathoms of ocean to where the *Titanic* was resting, her lights still blazing, her dead gazing out of her portholes. I scaled an ice mountain and met a black crow, who showed me the nest of white knuckle-bones where her seven rotten eggs were lying; never to hatch. I followed tunnels with no exits, climbed ladders to the dusty stars, experienced the terror of infinity beyond them. And I sat alone in a great wilderness, where the red eyes of wolves waited in a circle for the last, dim embers of my little campfire to die. The last thing I remember was hearing Tina's voice out there in the infinite darkness, crying out like a drowning sailor.

It shocked me, and I propped myself up on hands that had lost all feeling. The black crow's wings were beating around my head. Then one of the wolves shot out of the darkness and knocked me flat. There was no struggle left in me. I remember giving up; that extraordinary sense of abandonment, and the lack of fear as I waited for the beast's teeth to take that final, deadly grip on my throat.

But it didn't come. Instead a warm, wet tongue licked the frozen drips off my nose, and a voice that sounded like a panting breath said, 'Christie, Christie, Christie, Christie, Christie.'

It wasn't a wolf. It was Oggy.

part
six

one

'How on earth did you find us?' I said.

'Picked up your scent in the snow,' said Oggy. 'Been tracking you for hours.'

I hugged him tight. 'Fair play to you, Oggy. Fair play to you.'

He licked my face again, then squirmed out of my grasp. 'Darling has found a shed,' he said. 'Got to get the others up.'

He was already working on Danny, who sat up, saying, 'What? What?'

'Are you OK, Danny?' I said.

'Fine,' said Danny. ''Lo, Oggy.'

The space-blanket had served him well, and he seemed in better fettle than I was.

'Up you get,' I said. 'We're on the road again.' I got up, all my limbs numb, and started to help him to his feet. But then I saw something which sent a hot shock through my cold blood. Oggy was snuffling and scratching and whining around Tina's face, but he wasn't getting any response. She was showing no signs of life at all.

I couldn't believe it. Not Tina. She was the street kid; the tough one; the survivor among us. That's what I had always assumed, anyway. But I hadn't taken into account the effect that years of hardship and under-nourishment can have on the human body. Tina was wiry and strong, but she hadn't an ounce of spare flesh, and in conditions like these, she had no resistance at all.

I knelt down and felt for the pulse at her throat.

'She's OK,' I said. 'She'll be OK.' But it was more for my own benefit than anyone else's. I was terrified.

I shook her hard. 'Come on, Tina. Get up. We have to get up.'

She turned and moaned. I could just make out the flicker of her eyelids in the darkness.

'Oggy's here, Tina. We have to get up.'

'Oggy?' she said. 'Oggy doggy.' She sounded like a drunk.

'Come on, Tina.'

My fingers felt huge and useless, but I managed to make them grip her arm.

'Up, Tina. Up.'

I pulled, but she was like a sack of potatoes. I remem-bered hearing her voice calling out in my dream. But she wasn't going to die. Not if I could help it. I knelt in the snow, grabbed her by the shoulders, and shook her as hard as I could.

'Nooo,' she moaned. 'I'm tired. Leave me alone.'

'Get up, Tina. Get up.'

I hauled her up again, and this time she found some energy somewhere and helped. Danny had got himself up, and came to my assistance. He grabbed Tina's other arm and between us we succeeded in getting her to her feet.

'Come on,' Darling sang, somewhere off to our right. 'This way.'

Oggy went after her, to blaze the trail for us. I slung one of Tina's arms around my shoulders, and Danny took the other side. We staggered along for a few steps, but Danny was too unsteady in the snow and Tina cried out as her arms got wrenched apart.

'I'll take her, Danny,' I said. 'You get the blankets.'

He gathered them and went on ahead, lumbering like a walrus through the drifts, and I tried to keep in his foot-steps. Tina wasn't quite a dead weight, but she didn't seem to know where she was. Her head kept dropping on to my shoulder, as though she wanted to sleep. But I couldn't let her. I stopped, and shook her again, then slapped her across the face.

'Ow!' She flailed at me with both arms.

'That's it, Tina,' I said. 'Give me a box.'

But she just slumped against me again, and would have fallen if I hadn't held her up.

In the end I had to practically carry her. Ahead of us I could see Oggy's tail flying up and down as he bounded through the drifts. Behind him, Danny floundered and fell, but got himself up again, and ploughed on.

'Where is this blasted shed?' I called out. But no one answered. They just kept going. For an awful moment the snow tempted me. It would have been so easy, so comfortable, to go Tina's way instead of mine; to slide down into the sleepy cold and let it take us. Life was such a struggle. My eyelids drooped.

'No,' I said, aloud, as if Death were in the air around me. 'No, no, no.'

I hitched Tina's arm more tightly around my neck, and stumbled on.

two

There was a house there as well, but it had been abandoned for years and had no roof. But the shed was in good condition. It had been used to store hay for the upland cattle, and there were still quite a few bales left. I set about making a nest for us, and soon we were all bundled up in it. Danny and I lay one on either side of Tina, and Oggy sprawled across the top. We pulled the space-blanket over the lot of us, and tucked it in at the edges.

It wasn't until I felt the heat of our bodies beginning to collect in the insulated space that I realised how close to death we had been. Only then did my body begin to shake.

In the morning, Oggy and I retraced our tracks and retrieved the rest of our gear. I noticed that he had a piece of frayed rope tied around his neck, and I took it off for him. But when I asked him how it had got there, he just snarled and shook himself, and then snapped at the snow as if it was alive.

The food had suffered from being frozen, but it was all we

had, and we eked it out over the three days that we were snowed in up there on the mountain-side.

For the first day, Tina was still very shaky. She slept a lot, had no appetite, and her colour was always shifting; sometimes pale, sometimes beetroot red. She improved as time went on, but it was quite a while before she returned to her usual, carefree self. Danny, on the other hand, was doing really well, despite the frustration of having to stay so still. I saw that the journey was changing him, giving a purpose, perhaps, to his previously purposeless life. But I didn't know what it was doing to me. I found that I was torn between a fierce curiosity about Danny's mother, and a powerful desire to return to the familiarity and security of home. If there had been a phone, I would have called Mom; I would have shopped us all, for the possibility of being safe. But there wasn't, and those fiercely decisive moments always passed, and the other side would start to assert itself all over again. What was Maggie doing up there in Bettyhill? What could she do in her lab that would make animals talk? And what was she supposed to have done to Danny, which made him the way he was? I wanted to know so badly, but I couldn't see any way in the world of getting to Bettyhill, right up there in the north; light years away.

And then I would start thinking about home again.

I was in that kind of mood when I tried to get some support from Tina. Danny had gone out for a pee, and Oggy and Darling were out scouting, trying to plan a route for when the thaw came. I knew Tina was still feeling pretty poorly, and I felt like a bit of a heel as I started to speak.

'If you came home with us, Mom and Maurice would let you stay. You could be part of our family.'

She tried to look shocked and horrified, but I could tell that there was a bit of her, the vulnerable bit, that really liked the idea. I pushed my advantage.

'You're practically our sister now, aren't you? After all we've been through together.'

For an instant I knew she was with me, longing to be part of a family with a permanent, secure home. But then I saw her close down, as though the hope itself was too much to bear.

'You've got to be joking,' she said.

three

We had plenty of time for talking. Oggy eventually told us the story of how he had escaped from the man in the car; how the man had tried to tie him to a concrete block and drown him in the river.

'I wanted to bite his filthy hands off,' he said, and Darling said 'Yay, Oggy!'

'I didn't succeed, I'm afraid. Once I got nasty he moved pretty fast, back towards the car. I had to chew my way through the rope, but at least I was free.

'I had a lot of adventures,' Oggy went on. 'I got shot at by a farmer and I killed a rabbit and ate it, brains and all. Then I got buzzed by a gang of starlings and they steered me north west. I thought they might be pals of yours, Darling, so I took their advice.'

Darling gave Tina a long look, but for once, she wasn't ready with a snappy comment.

'That's all, really,' said Oggy. 'I followed that big main road, and I found a car where you had clearly spent some time. Then I just followed your trail.'

'But didn't the snow cover our tracks?' I said.

'Of course,' said Oggy. 'But you can see a lot with your nose, if you know how.'

Danny snorted. 'See with your nose,' he said.

'I might talk,' said Oggy, sourly. 'But I'm still a dog.'

I hugged him tight and looked into his eyes. They were full of obsequious devotion, but after a moment he turned away, and as he did so I caught a glimpse of something else there; something darker that lay concealed beneath the friendly surface. It troubled me, and I did my best to put it out of my mind.

four

On the morning of the fourth day we packed up and set out again. The going was still heavy, but the snow was softening and we could hear the trickle of meltwater running beneath it. Oggy found rabbit tracks and quartered around, snuffling and being macho. But he didn't find anything, and we continued on our way as hungry as before.

For the whole of the day we slogged on through the slushy snow, and when we failed to find anywhere safe to sleep, we slogged on through the night as well. In the morning of the following day, we reached Aviemore, where troops of stranded skiers stood waiting for buses, looking gloomy despite their colourful gear.

The food shops were all closed, but there was a tourist shop near the bus stop, and we all slouched in. We each bought gloves and scarves and thick, hiking socks, and we stocked up on Edinburgh rock, slabs of mint-cake and fudge in tartan boxes.

I had had more than enough of walking, and plenty of time to make a plan. I intended to book us into a B&B, then find a phone and settle in to wait until Mom and Maurice arrived. I didn't know how they'd get there, and it occurred to me that they might even leave it to the police to pick us up. I didn't care any more. Anything had to be better than hunger and exhaustion.

But things didn't go according to plan. As soon as we emerged from the shop, Oggy got lured into a fight by a belligerent mastiff, and before we could separate them a bus pulled in with INVERNESS written across its brow.

The skiers, like dancers, leant out from the pavement, read the destination of the bus, and leant back dejectedly. Tina grabbed me by the arm.

'It's our bus!' she said.

'Our bus. Our bus!' said Danny, forgetting about chocolate and wading rashly in to drag Oggy out of his fight.

'But I want . . .' I began. Then my heart sank, as once again events conspired against me. The bus pulled up, and Tina and Danny were already beside it, with Oggy, still bristling, close behind. A few dozen people were getting off, looking sleepy and dishevelled, but there wasn't a big crowd getting on and I had no choice but to join the others. Darling swept down from the rooftops and into my pocket and Tina, always the sharpest among us, had the presence of mind to take off her coat and drape it over her bag so that Oggy could hide underneath it.

The conductor stood with his back to the driver and confronted us like a bouncer.

'Where are you going?' he barked.

'Inverness,' said Tina.

'What for?'

'We're going home.'

'Address?' he demanded.

'Bettyhill,' I said.

'Bettyhill?' said the conductor. 'There'll be no bus this day to Bettyhill!'

But Tina's wits were about her. 'Our mother is meeting us in Inverness.'

'You have funny accents for Bettyhill,' said the conductor. 'Let's see some I.D.'

We looked at each other.

'Come on let's have it,' he went on. 'New regulations. Essential journeys only.'

I was sure that our bus ride wasn't going to happen after all, but Tina was still on the ball.

'We're all in boarding school in Ireland,' she said.

'Boarding school in Ireland?' The conductor laughed, and so did the driver. 'What are they teaching you there? Hod carrying?'

My blood boiled. I was suddenly determined to get on that bus, even though I didn't want to. 'I'll have you know,' I said, 'that the Irish education system . . .'

'All right, all right,' said the conductor. 'I don't believe it for a minute, but you get ten out of ten for the story.'

He issued our tickets, but I wasn't ready to give up yet. As

I handed him the money, I said, 'Ireland's main export these days is brains.'

'I'm sure of it,' he said, sorting out my change. 'All ground up and made into sausages.'

I was still fuming as we went down the aisle and filled the back seats, but we were aboard, and that was what mattered.

five

And in Inverness, we got our own back. When we got off the bus with Oggy in full view beside us, it was the conductor's turn to go red in the face.

'Hey,' he spluttered. 'Who said you could bring that dog on the bus!'

'But it's off we're bringing him, surr,' I said, in my best stage-Irish brogue.

And Tina said, 'Bejasus it's the dog. 'Twas the pig I thought I was hiding!'

We tumbled on to the footpath and Danny's toneless laughter made everyone stare, which made us crease up even harder. We laughed until our ribs ached and our eyes ran. But it was the last laugh we were to have for quite a while.

Because Inverness was a nightmare.

There were soldiers in the streets, hugging their rifles to their chests like precious toys. Young men in small groups hurled abuse at them in accents too thick for me to understand. It reminded me of Belfast during the Troubles, except that this was worse, because it wasn't all safely on television. I was like Chauncey Gardener in *Being There*. I wanted to point my remote and switch them all off. But these soldiers were real and their guns were not new and shiny, but worn and well-used.

To my horror, Tina showed her usual disregard for authority. She marched up to a young soldier who was leaning against a wall and said, 'What's going on?'

When he didn't answer she turned on the charm, showing him her empty hands and making 'help me' faces.

'Civil unrest,' he said at last, turning away from her. 'Peace-keeping duties. Now clear off.'

We cleared off and, foolishly, followed the signs for the City Centre. I think we had an idea that we might find a café or a supermarket. But all we found was trouble.

The first crowd we came across were queuing for bread. Above the assembled heads we could see the high sides of a pantechnicon. It was plastered with notices saying: ONLY ONE LOAF PER HEAD and ONE POUND PER LOAF. Ahead of us we saw a small child drop a pound coin and scramble for it among the milling feet. Quicker than a flash, Darling darted in and retrieved it, and Tina dropped it into the astonished child's hand.

Despite our lack of provisions, we quickly ruled out joining the bread queue. We decided to retrace our steps to the bus station, and took a side street leading away from the crowds. But halfway down it we ran into more trouble.

A soldier was harassing a woman who had somehow managed to get hold of several of the rationed loaves. We were watching in a kind of shocked stupor when a group of lads came to her rescue and began pelting the soldier with stones. He lowered his rifle. Danny clutched my arm, and Oggy dived into another side street. We followed, Tina and I, crouching instinctively and drawing Danny down with us.

There was no firing, but we didn't turn back. Instead we kept going, away from the centre and the bus station, heading for anywhere that might be free of mobs and soldiers. But in no time at all we ran into more trouble.

Darling, keeping a lookout from the air, dropped down to warn us.

'Looks bad,' she whispered. 'Big crowds approaching.'

'From where?' I said.

'From everywhere,' she said. 'I can't see any way out.'

'More bread queues?' I asked. But it wasn't. A moment later, we were in the middle of it. Angry multitudes were marching on the town centre behind banners which read: SCOTLAND IS STARVING and WE DEMAND RESPONSIBLE GOVERNMENT.

A television crew with a hand-held camera hopped backwards ahead of the marchers and nearly collided with us as we glued ourselves to the wall. As they squeezed past us, people trod on our feet and kicked our ankles, and Oggy got dribbled along like a football for several metres before he managed to break free and weave his way back.

I was worried about Danny, but he didn't seem to be bothered by the crowds. He was smiling at everyone he met and offering them handshakes. Some people steered clear, put off by his strange appearance. But others smiled back and shook his offered hand heartily.

Tina grabbed a woman by the elbow and asked her what was happening.

'It's those fat slobs in Edinburgh,' she said, pointing down at the ground as though the fat slobs were already being roasted in fire and brimstone. 'They call themselves a government but they couldn't run a dog show. There are mountains of food in the south, but the Highlands and Islands are starving!' She was being jostled by the people behind her and her last words were called out to us as she reversed away.

'Look at the soldiers! We might as well still be ruled by Westminster!'

Then her words were drowned, as a great roar went up somewhere behind us. I guessed that the mob had run into the bread queues and I could only imagine what the result might have been. All I knew for certain was that I wanted to be out of there. The protesters were slowing down as the head of the march came to a stop, and the crush was becoming dangerous. I grabbed Danny's coat and, clinging to the wall, began to forge a slow escape.

It was as tiring as swimming through mud. When I ran out of steam, Tina took over, and whether the crowds were thinner by then or whether she just used her elbows more viciously, I don't know. But we certainly made faster progress. Eventually, bruised and weary, we succeeded in reaching the back of the march.

We plonked ourselves down on the kerb. Above the rooftops a helicopter swung back and forth, surveying the crowd.

'There's always fuel for those things,' said Tina, scowling up at it. 'Any chance of a lift, Mister? Go flag him down, Darling!'

But none of us felt like laughing.

'We should have stayed at the bus depot,' I said. 'We should have waited till we could get a bus going south.'

'South?' said Tina. 'I thought we were going north.'

'We were,' I said. 'But there's no point, is there? You heard what that woman said. There's no food.'

'We have food,' said Danny, optimistic as a small child, and, I realised, as innocent.

'These are sweets, not food,' I said, waving my plastic bag. 'You know, there really isn't any alternative. We'll have to go back.'

'I'm never going back,' said Tina.

'Never going back,' parroted Danny.

'But you nearly died already!' I barked at Tina. 'Do you want to try again? Up there in the middle of nowhere? Is that what you want?'

Tina just shrugged, and Oggy, infuriatingly, licked her face approvingly. I turned to Danny instead.

'I don't know why you want to go, anyway. You had

165

everything you wanted at home. Everyone bent over back-wards for you. What do you think your mother can do for you that Mom or Maurice can't? Eh?'

Danny looked me straight in the eye, and what he said seemed to come from a clear place deep within; a place where he wasn't an innocent child, but a suffering young man approaching adulthood.

'Mother's going to show me what I am,' he said.

I was so frustrated that I wanted to tell him what he was: a top-heavy shambling freak, whose only worthwhile quality was a weird skill at holding his breath. But I couldn't summon the cruelty to do it, and instead I got up and walked towards a block of phone boxes I had spotted at the end of the street.

I would have done it. I would have told them where we were, got them to pick us up or set the police on us, even the army. But the blasted line was dead. I tried another box, then another. They were all dead. Maybe there was a communications blackout because of the trouble. Or maybe it was worse. Maybe there would never be any phones again.

part
seven

one

This time there would be no hiding for Danny; no turning away and pretending it wasn't there. It was broad daylight, now, and the sea was vast and bright.

We were barely out of Inverness when it came into view. Danny stopped dead in his tracks and stared. I stopped beside him and put a hand on his arm. His entire attention was taken, and his face registered acute anxiety. For a long, long time he stood there, and I was afraid to break his mesmerised state in case I nudged him the wrong way, over into a wobbler. But in the end I had to do something.

'Come on, Danny,' I said. 'It's just the sea. Let's get on, shall we?'

I mightn't have been there, for all the notice he took of me. He continued to stare, and I saw, or maybe I just sensed, that every one of his nerve-ends was taut and trembling.

A car passed and Tina tried to thumb it, without success. Danny didn't even see it. The breeze was fresh and kept changing its mind about where it was going, so the waves were hitting the shore with an irregular sloshing sound.

'Just the waves,' I said to Danny. 'Hear them? Whoosh, whoosh.'

'They can't get you,' said Tina. 'They're stuck on the beach, see?'

Abruptly, Danny's trance broke. He took a few faltering steps, then shied away violently and began to run along the edge of the road, making a distressed keening sound. I was certain he was about to loop the loop in a major way, but his attention was beyond my reach and there was nothing I could do but follow. He turned back, bumbling along the other way, and Tina and I followed again, calling uselessly after him. Again he turned, running along the road but looking the other way; out to sea.

I caught up with him. 'What is it, Danny?' I said.

He stopped, finally, and looked at me. His expression was full of anguish, like nothing I'd ever seen on his face before.

'The big sea, Christie,' he said. 'People can't live in it.'

'That's right,' I said. 'Not for long, anyway. But it can't hurt you, Danny. It can't come out of its bed.'

I don't know if he heard me. 'Can't live in it,' he repeated, apprehensively. 'Can't live in it.'

two

For four days we trudged northwards. Few cars passed us and no buses. Not going our way, anyway. It soon became clear that the majority of traffic was headed south, and that we were swimming against the tide.

The sweets and biscuits gave us little bursts of energy but minimal nourishment, and by the end of the third day, even they were gone. Our bodies began drawing upon their reserves and produced a kind of deep, urgent hunger that I had never experienced before. Danny was the least affected, since he had more fat to live off. But I had no idea where Tina was getting the strength to continue.

In desperation, we took to begging at houses along the way. All we got in return for our humiliation was more of it; suspicion, rejection and hostility. No one had food to spare.

In the afternoon of the fourth day, a fine drizzle began which soaked us to the bone. When we spotted a house standing back off the road, we made a bee-line for it.

It was Tina's turn to knock. We waited, but no one answered. Tina knocked again, a bit harder. There was still no reply, but Oggy brought news from around the back.

'There's no one there,' he said. 'But there's a stack of wood in the shed.'

'That's useful,' said Tina, caustically.

'It is,' said Oggy. 'And you never know what we might find inside.'

At that moment Darling appeared around the side of the house. She had something in her bill, which she dropped carefully into my hand. It was a key.

My protestations about illegal entry were quickly over-ruled, and a minute later we were inside. The cottage was damp and musty, as though it had been empty for a long time, but there was a fire already set in the fireplace, waiting for the occupants to return.

Our matches were damp, but I found a lighter on the mantelpiece and set the fire-lighters blazing. Meanwhile, Tina and Oggy were searching through the kitchen cupboards, looking for something to eat. But there was nothing. Nothing at all. Whoever lived here had taken everything with them when they left.

'At least we'll get warm,' I said. But my heart was in my boots as I said it. We needed more than heat if we were to survive.

We made the most of the fire, spreading out our gear to dry and airing the damp blankets we found in a cupboard. But our spirits were low and we couldn't find anything to talk about. As soon as it was dark, we took ourselves up to the little, wood-walled bedrooms and settled down to sleep.

three

I was woken at first light by Oggy licking my face.

'Get up, Christie,' he whispered.

'Why?' I said.

'We have to get food. You have to help me.'

I slipped out of the bed I was sharing with Danny and got dressed without waking him. As we crept downstairs, Oggy told me to go to the kitchen and fetch a sharp knife.

'What for?' I said.

But he just said, 'Shh!' and went on ahead of me to the back door.

'I don't like this,' I said to him. 'What's the knife for, Oggy?'

He made me let him out before he answered, and then his words made my skin crawl.

'These are jungle days, Christie,' he said. 'We can sit down and wait for our deaths or we can go out and profit from someone else's.'

He trotted across the bare vegetable patch and, reluctantly, I followed. I remembered his evasiveness the time I had tried to look into his eyes, and now I knew that there had been something he had been trying to hide. But I didn't know what.

'Are you planning on murdering someone?' I hissed.

'I might call it murder,' he said. 'But you wouldn't. I'm going to get us a sheep.'

'But we can't!'

'Why not?'

'Because they belong to the farmer!' I said.

'He has hundreds of them,' said Oggy. 'Would you die before you'd steal?'

'No,' I said. 'No, I wouldn't. But I can't kill something. I don't know how!'

'That's OK,' said Oggy. 'I do.'

He hopped over the garden wall and I made a less dignified crossing behind him. I could just make out flat grey fields beyond, stretching to the horizon. My heart was doing somersaults as we walked over the first of them, but nothing moved. We crossed a second field, and then a third, and the blue-grey light leaked into the darkness around us. At the next wall, Oggy stood on his hind legs and peered over, then ducked back and waited for me to catch up.

'Stay here,' he said. 'And whatever you do, don't make a sound.'

There was a business-like tone to his voice that troubled me. He was normally so cooperative and eager to please that I had considered myself to be his superior. In our world, under our rules, perhaps I was. But that day, in the no-man's time of dawn, there was no doubt about who was in command.

While I watched, he poured himself over the wall and slid along the edge of the field like a shadow. From where I stood I could see the sheep lying on the ground in the shelter of a tall hedge. Despite Oggy's quiet approach, they spotted him early and rose to their feet to face him.

He stopped and, feigning indifference, sniffed the air and lifted his leg against the wall. Then he trotted off at an angle, as if he were heading for the opposite corner of the field. The sheep kept their eyes on him, turning their bodies instead of their heads, always face-on to the threat. Oggy went as far as the wall, then snuffled around some more and turned back. This time his trajectory brought him much closer to the anxious flock, and they began to shrink backwards away from him.

He stopped and sniffed the air again, looking languidly around at everything except the sheep. They peered out mistrustfully, and a ewe in the foreground stamped her front foot; a nervous tick disguised as a threat. Oggy trotted forward again, as though he couldn't care less. And then, like lightning, he struck.

The startled sheep scattered explosively, but for one of them it was already too late. Oggy had her by the throat and nothing could make him let go. For a few yards she stayed on her feet, dragging Oggy along with her, his paws digging for purchase in the soft ground. Then he got it and, with a desperate bleat, the ewe went down.

Dogs barked in the distance, but my heart couldn't beat any faster without bursting. The sheep was thrashing wildly, but Oggy dodged her feet and maintained his lethal grip. While her companions regrouped and looked on, her struggles diminished and then, with one final convulsion, they stopped.

I was glued to the spot, and I didn't move until Oggy began dragging the heavy carcass over the ground towards me. I got over the wall, knocking down a few stones and setting the distant farm dogs barking again. Praying that their owner wouldn't heed them, I ran across to help bring in the catch.

Oggy was bristling with pride.

'See that, eh?' he jabbered, still in top gear. 'The speed of it, eh? She never knew what hit her.'

'Where's the blood?' I asked, grabbing a fistful of warm fleece and hauling the limp carcass towards home.

'I choked her,' said Oggy. 'Pick her up, will you? Carry her!'

I crouched down and fed the front legs over my shoulders, then lifted her up like a sack. She was heavy, but manageable.

The farm dogs were howling like wolves and Oggy raced

nervously backwards and forwards between me and the wall.

'Hurry up, Christie,' he said. 'If you get caught you might get a hefty fine. But if they catch me, there's no trial, you know. Instant execution.'

We made it to the wall and tipped the sheep over. Oggy pounced on her as though he intended to kill her all over again.

'Come on, come on,' he said. 'The sun will be up in a minute.'

I was fagged out by the time we dropped her over the garden wall, but the worst bit hadn't begun, yet.

'Dig a hole there where the ground is bare,' said Oggy, still in the general's role.

'What for? Are we going to bury her now?'

'Just the bits we don't want,' he said. 'The evidence.'

I was weak as a kitten after the long days without food, but I used what strength I had economically and the ground was easy enough to dig. While I worked, Oggy dragged the ewe over and parked her beside the hole. When he considered it deep enough, he told me to get out the knife. I took it from my pocket and felt the edge. It was soft steel, sharpened like a razor.

'Open her up,' said Oggy.

My knees went weak. 'Open her up?' I said.

Oggy gave me a look, and in a tone that cut as deep as any knife, he said, 'Welcome to the real world, Christie.'

I took a deep breath and got to work. As the guts spilt into the hole, Oggy snatched the liver and gobbled it down like a pelican. The darkness I had seen in him was in every one of his actions now. I felt that I hardly knew him.

I loosened the hide with the knife and Oggy hauled it clear of the muscle and bone beneath. He was still hyper, snapping and worrying at the skin as if it were alive. His aggression, his raw strength frightened me, and I knew that I would treat him with less fluff and more respect from now on.

We needed a hatchet to finish the job, and luckily there was one in the wood shed. Afterwards, I filled in the hole, washed the blood off my hands and Oggy's coat, and went in to present the others with breakfast.

four

I didn't regret killing that sheep. How could I, when she kept us alive? There was no doubt in my mind that we would never have got to Bettyhill without the meat she provided for us.

But Oggy's harsh words about the real world had hurt because they had hit upon a truth. I had never questioned the lumps of meat that appeared on my plate every dinner time at home. I thought that vegetarians were sissies and that butchers were smiling men in white coats and funny hats. And as for slaughterhouses, I never thought about them at all.

But now I did. As we cooked the ragged lumps of meat over the open fire I thought about more as well; about how almost all of the food that used to come into our house was processed and packaged and turned into something it hadn't been before it started. I thought about all the machines and packaging plants that were needed to do all of that, and the fuel it took to run them. And then I wondered where all the madness had started and whether the new madness had brought about its end.

I turned my attention back to the pan. I wasn't great shakes as a butcher. The meat was in big, funny-shaped chunks and they were sticking to the pan and giving off clouds of acrid smoke. When we came to eat it, it was black on the outside, red on the inside, and tough as old shoe leather. But it was food.

We decided to stay on for the rest of the day and make use of the fire. We ate all we could manage and cooked more over the fire for the journey. In the afternoon Tina found the electricity box, and switched on the power. For a while we used the oven instead, until a power cut turned us off again. By evening we had a good supply of cold, roast mutton, and the last of it we planned to carry raw, because Oggy said he preferred his that way. Danny and I were rooting around in the kitchen for something to wrap it all in, when suddenly the phone rang.

The phone. I hadn't even seen it. Before I had worked out where it was, Tina had answered it.

'Hello?'

There was a pause, and then she said, 'Sorry. Wrong number.'

She put it down.

'You idiot,' I said. 'Why did you answer it?'

'Because it rang,' said Tina.

'But now someone knows we're here.'

'So what?'

'So we shouldn't be, that's what!'

The phone started ringing again, and this time we left it, and it finally shut up. But Tina didn't.

'I'm sick to death of you, Mr Goody-Two-Shoes, always "should this" and "shouldn't that". I don't know how I'm going to stand living with you if we ever get to this stupid place!'

She stood up and stormed out of the house. Oggy looked at me and, with a kind of canine shrug, he followed her.

Tina's outburst was unsettling, but the presence of the phone was more so. I sat and looked at it for twenty minutes, while Danny amused himself by poking little twigs into the fire and watching them burn. How long was it since we had left? A week? A month? I couldn't remember, and in any case, that kind of time had no meaning now that it was no longer tied to school hours and television listings.

'Let's phone home, Danny,' I said.

'Yeah,' he said, guileless as ET. 'Phone home.'

I reached for the handset and dialled.

'Christie?' said Mom.

'Hi, Mom,' I said, but her voice was still coming down the line. 'If that's you, please leave a message for us, will you? We've had to go out for a while, but we'll be back, soon. Please phone again, Christie, won't you?'

There was a click and a bleep, and then silence.

'The answer-phone,' I told Danny. I put it down, then rang it again, just to hear her voice. But I couldn't bring myself to talk on to the tape, not the way I felt just then.

I threw a few logs on to the fire and watched the woodlice trying to escape, but I kept thinking about the answer-phone talking in the empty house, pouring out Mom's sorrow, again and again and again. I wondered how long it had been there. Hours? Days? What if they had intended to come back and hadn't made it? What if our town was like Inverness; hungry and dangerous?

I couldn't bear my thoughts and, desperate for company, I went looking for Oggy and Tina. They weren't far away. I found them in the tiny wood shed, sheltering from an icy shower. I squeezed into a corner and sat on an upturned bucket.

'Get lost,' said Tina. 'I don't want to talk to you.'

I didn't have the energy to argue, but I wasn't going to leave, either.

'Come on, you two,' said Darling. She was up in the narrow roof somewhere, invisible in the windowless gloom. 'Kiss and make up.'

Tina picked up a small log and lobbed it up into the beams. Darling squawked like a chicken.

'Sorry!' she said. 'It's just something Mother says when people are scrapping.'

'Do you know something?' said Tina. 'I'm sick of hearing about Mother. Mother this, Mother that. She sounds more like a Fairy Godmother, if you ask me.'

She tore a piece of bark from a block of firewood and, as she spoke, broke bits of it off and flicked them at the door.

'You know what gets me about all this?' she went on. 'What kind of a woman abandons a baby of six months old and then wants him back fifteen years later? When someone else has done all the work and paid all the bills?'

'Well,' said Darling, defensively. 'It's just that Mother . . . well, Mother . . .'

'Mother what?' said Tina. 'If my mother sent for me now I'd tell her to take a running jump, so I would.'

Oggy made the connection quicker than I did.

'Did your mother leave you as well?' he asked.

'She did, as a matter of fact,' said Tina. 'Not that I care.'

But she clearly did. Oggy licked her chin and Darling made soft, sympathetic whistles.

'We're all in the same boat, so,' I said. 'My dad left me as well. How old were you?'

But Tina had said enough. 'I'm not telling my life story, here. And I don't want to hear yours, all right? I'm just telling you why I'm not thrilled about absent mothers, that's all.'

'I thought it was men you didn't like,' I said. 'Sounds like you don't like anybody.'

'Oh, bog off, Christie,' said Tina. She wrapped her arms round Oggy and held him tight.

five

The mutton was heavy in the borrowed bags, but it sustained us, and over the next couple of days we made good time. On the morning of the third day, we reached a little town called Altnaharra where, to our surprise, the door of the post office stood open. It gave me an idea and we went in.

An old lady was sitting at the counter, knitting. She displayed no surprise at our appearance, and finished the row she was on before giving me her attention.

'Is the post still going?' I asked.

'It is and it isn't,' she replied. 'Where are ye heading?'

'Bettyhill,' I said.

'Well, then,' she said. 'The post is going to Bettyhill.' She began rooting through a neat file of letters and pulled three of them out. 'Are ye going by Tongue or by Syre and Skail?'

I thought they must be obscure Scottish forms of transport, and looked over to Tina for help. But the postmistress cleared up the matter.

'Are ye on foot?'

'We are,' I said.

'Then Syre and Skail is your best road.' She rummaged again, found four more letters and a small parcel, then handed the lot over the counter to me. I looked at them in bewilderment, but Tina was ahead of me.

'We have to deliver them, thicko,' she said. 'We're Irish,' she went on, as though it explained everything.

'And you want to send a letter home, I'll warrant,' said the woman. 'I can't guarantee it, ye ken. But there are plenty of folk going south and I'll get it as far as I can.'

She held out her hand for my letter.

'I haven't written it yet,' I admitted, beginning to wonder if it was such a good idea after all.

'Ah, bless you,' she said. 'I've plenty of paper and envelopes. Or would you rather a postcard? I have nice ones for sale.'

'Just a letter, I think,' I said.

While I chewed on the end of the pen and tried to get my thoughts in order, the post-mistress chatted to Tina and Danny.

'Strange talk coming down from Bettyhill these days,' she said. 'Very strange talk.'

'What kind of strange talk would that be?' asked Tina. Butter wouldn't melt in her mouth.

I chewed some more on the pen, and a bit of the plastic

broke off in my mouth. Maybe I should have gone for the card after all.

'Weird children living up there,' said the old woman. 'And animals talking. Some say it's a sign of the end of the world.'

Oggy sat looking innocent and utterly dumb beside the door. By now my mind was a total blank. Recklessly, I wrote the first thing that came into my head: *WISH YOU WERE HERE!!! Luv from Christie and Danny xxxx*. Then I scrumpled it up and shoved it into the envelope.

Tina was saying, 'I wouldn't believe any of that old chat if I were you.' I handed the letter over the counter, and the postmistress turned a withering look from Tina to me.

'Here in Scotland,' she said, 'we usually put a name and address on the front.'

Blushing with shame, I addressed the letter and paid for a stamp. But the old woman's confidence in us had been somewhat eroded.

'You'll be sure to deliver those letters, now, won't you?' she said. 'Would you like me to read you the addresses?'

'It's all right,' I said.

'We promise,' said Tina.

'Syre and Skail!' the postmistress called after us as we tumbled back out on to the street.

A few miles later we stopped to gnaw on some more of the mutton. Oggy was uneasy.

'I don't like those rumours,' he said. 'I don't know how they could be getting out.'

'What was that about the weird children?' I asked. But Oggy slunk off with his share of meat and didn't answer.

As we ate, Darling spied out the land. We had taken the turning for Syre and Skail and were walking beside the long shore of Loch Naver. By our reckoning it was not much more than twenty miles to Bettyhill, and with luck we would reach there tomorrow. The day had been clear and the waters were blue as the sky, but in the short time it took us to eat, they changed to an ochrish grey. When Darling returned she was worried. Behind her, the sky had gone black.

'Another blizzard,' she said. 'And it's coming in fast.'

We all drew in to try and decide what to do. Darling and I were for holing up somewhere and sitting out the storm, but the others were afraid we'd get snowed in for the winter and favoured pushing on through. We were all so intent upon our deliberations that no one noticed the new arrival until a voice said, 'Is that you, Oggy?'

Oggy's head went up so fast that he hit me in the jaw and made my teeth crack like a gunshot.

On the shore of the lake stood a huge, white bird. I could tell it was a seabird of some kind, but it was bigger than any gull I had ever seen.

'Albert,' said Oggy.

'Albert,' said Darling.

They both sprang at the white bird, and for a few terrifying moments the rest of us witnessed a lurching, flapping tussle of monstrous wings and flying fur. Little Darling vanished altogether in the frenzy, but when the action eventually ceased, all three of them emerged unscathed.

'I've been looking for you for weeks,' said Albert, stretching and refolding his enormous wings. 'Mother has almost given up on you.'

'Tough road,' said Oggy. 'Tough mission.'

Albert surveyed us carefully with one dark eye, and then with the other. 'I was never very good at counting,' he said. 'But I think there's more than two of them there.'

'You're right,' said Oggy. 'There are three.'

'Three,' said Albert. 'That's a lot, isn't it?'

'No,' said Oggy. 'It's only one more than two.'

Albert nodded gravely. 'Are they nice ones?' he asked.

It was strange, being talked about like that, as though we were cattle Albert was thinking of buying.

'We've got ears, you know,' I called. 'And we can talk as well.'

'Of course,' said Albert, slightly flustered. 'Of course you can. And very nicely, too.'

He was stupid, I decided. A big, stupid waddling lump of a thing.

'What'll we do?' Oggy was saying. 'About this blizzard, I mean. Should we wait or keep going?'

'You'd better keep going,' said Albert. 'I'll go on ahead and tell them you're coming.'

Oggy and Darling returned to us, and we all watched as Albert walked slowly over to the road.

'What's he doing?' I asked.

'He just needs a bit of a runway,' said Oggy.

'A runway?' said Tina. 'What kind of a bird is he?'

'A goony bird,' said Darling.

'A goony bird?' I said. 'Why isn't he called Moony, then. Or Loony?'

Oggy didn't answer, and I didn't press him, because the entertainment had begun. With huge, reaching strides and flapping wings, Albert had begun to run along the tarmac. It was one of the funniest things I had ever seen; like an aeroplane with long legs instead of wheels.

'No wonder they call him a goony bird,' I said, bursting myself laughing. But the next moment, a completely different emotion overtook me, as the great wings found lift and he rose, with heart-stopping grace, into the skies. Just once he circled above us, the immense wings almost motionless, a perfection of airborne design.

'He honoured us, Christie,' said Darling. 'He rarely sets foot upon land.'

'Albert,' I said, watching him glide away effortlessly towards the north. 'Albert Ross.'

And then we were into the blizzard.

We made the best headway we could, and a few hours later we delivered the package to an astonished woman in Syre. By the time we reached Skail it was after dark, and we might have kept going all night if it wasn't for the other four letters.

'Just leave them,' said Tina. 'Just shove them through any old door.'

I was about to object, but the *Goody-Two-Shoes* charge had hurt. I said nothing, and we posted them through the door of the first lighted house we found. Before we had reached the end of the garden wall, a voice called out after us. An old man was standing in the doorway, peering at the letters.

'What's this?' he said.

We went back and I apologised.

'We didn't have time to find out where they were supposed to go,' I said.

He nodded, slowly, then said, 'You'd better come in.'

'No, thanks all the same,' said Tina. 'We just want to know where to take the letters.'

'I'll tak' them myself in the morning,' said the man. 'Come in, now, and out of that cold.'

'You're very kind,' said Tina, 'But we're on our way to Bettyhill and we won't stop now.'

The old man filled his lungs with night air and bellowed like a Highland warrior.

'No man, woman nor beast will go to Bettyhill this night. Not while I have a roof and a fire to share with them. Come in before I catch my death waiting on you, and bring your wee dog in as well.'

While the others traipsed inside, I hung back, waiting for Darling. She came to my outstretched arm, but she decided not to come in with us.

'I want to keep watch,' she said. 'I'm not sure why. I just have a feeling.'

I made a little tent by hanging my scarf over the handlebars of the old man's bike, which leant against the wall, and she roosted beneath it on the front mudguard. Then I followed the others inside.

At the old man's bright hearth we had strong, sweet tea; the first cup we'd had for a week. He told us he wouldn't leave Skail except in a coffin, and that most of the other villagers felt the same. He said that Scotland had survived worse challenges and that life would go on, come what may. Then he took himself and his little dog off to bed and left us to camp down beside the fire.

Darling's feeling proved to have substance. In the early hours of the morning she woke us, flapping at the window like a demented bat. I got up and opened it a crack. Snowflakes blew in on top of us.

'Get up, quick!' said Darling. 'Tony's here!'

'Tony?' I said, but she was gone, back into the snow-bound dark.

Between us, Oggy and I roused the others into action and then, still groggy with sleep, we stumbled out of the house.

There was nothing to be seen in the street except snow, but Darling came back for us and we followed her. Around the next bend stood the smartest little pony I had ever seen. He wasn't very big; his withers barely came up to my chest. But what there was of him was pure power. His shoulders were broad, his quarters were round with hard muscle, and the steam which rose from his sweating coat melted the snow as it fell. Best of all, he was harnessed to a neat little trap with a canvas hood to keep out the weather.

As we approached, his bright little eyes settled on Oggy and he snorted with glee.

'Hi there, dog face,' he said. 'What's the story?' His voice was strained and grunty, emerging before the pressure of a huge amount of breath.

'Hi, hobnail,' said Oggy, dancing up puffs of snow beneath Tony's nose. 'Can you handle us all in that thing?'

'Three people?' said Tony. 'No bother. But I don't carry dogs. You can walk.'

We took down the hood while we clambered aboard, then pulled it back over us again. The trap springs creaked and it seemed like an impossible load for Tony to pull. But as soon as we were all aboard, he swung round in the street and took off through the snow at a brisk trot.

'Dingle bells, dingle bells,' sang Danny, over and over again.

Through the rest of the night the pony laboured away, uphill and down, delighting in his own strength and wanting nothing more than to use it. The trap soon warmed up with the heat of our bodies, and the swaying and bouncing was hypnotic. Feeling safe at last, totally confident that Tony would get us to Bettyhill, I slipped down in my seat and closed my eyes. Before I fell asleep, I promised myself that I would, one day, retrace my steps, call on all the people who had been so kind to us along the way, and make my way home to Mom and Maurice.

part
eight

Somebody pulled back the hood and the morning light woke me. We were still moving, but more slowly now, and there was some kind of uproar ahead. I sat up and peered into the wirling blizzard. I could hear a babble of voices, all kinds of them: shrill, piping, gruff, blaring, sing-song, harsh. But when I saw who they belonged to, I nearly fell through the floor.

Like a dam-burst, the animals of Fourth World emerged from the white air and flowed around the trap on all sides of us. In the midst of them Oggy was a spiralling dervish, all but concealed by the explosions of snow he created. I lost sight of him as a mob of small creatures swarmed over Tony and jumped or clambered or flew into the trap. And all of them were talking.

It was overwhelming. Tina hid her face in her hands and squealed, but she was laughing at the same time. Danny spread his arms and got covered in birds; a snow-powdered, feathery angel.

There were finches and buntings, robins and magpies,

rabbits and rats and goats. All of them were bombarding us with greetings and questions:

'Welcome to Fourth World.'

'How old are you?'

'How far have you come?'

'Is that as big as you get?'

'Do you eat eggs?'

'Are you Sprog's brother?'

'Have you got sharp teeth?'

A large, pink mouse grabbed hold of my ear with his front paws and yelled into it at the top of his tiny voice. 'Are you a boy personality or a girl personality?'

While I was trying to work that one out, he set off into my underpants to find out for himself, and I had to haul him out by the tail.

'Don't you have any manners?' I said.

A small badger took him gently from me and they sat on the door of the trap discussing the difference between 'person' and 'personality'. Meanwhile, the questions continued.

'Have you got any children?'

'Are you house-trained yet?'

'How many is three?'

'Can you see colours?'

'Will you be staying in the house or the woods?'

'What's a personage, then?' I heard the pink mouse say to the badger.

'It's a place where a parson lives,' said the badger. And before I could set them straight, Oggy jumped in and knocked them both off the door, and they vanished among the heaving hordes on the floor.

Then Oggy jumped in again. Or that's what it looked like to me.

'This is my sister, Itchy,' he said. They were both wagging their tails so hard that several small birds and something that looked like the pink mouse got launched out into the blizzard again. I tried to give Itchy my attention, but a squirrel had just run up my sleeve and a persistent goat kid was throttling me with my scarf and saying, 'Can I borrow this? Can I borrow this?'

And then we had come to a stop, and Maggie was coming down the steps of Fourth World to meet us.

'How wonderful,' she kept saying. 'How wonderful.' A lot of the littlest voices joined in like tiny echoes. 'How wonderful. How wonderful. How wonderful!'

I was first out of the trap, and Maggie came forward to meet me.

'Hello, Christie,' she said. 'Good to see you again.'

She was exactly as I remembered her; tall, straight-backed, magnificently self-possessed. I had never come across a woman like her.

'Hello, M . . . Maggie,' I said, boldly, and all the little voices said, 'He's Christie. Christie. He called her Maggie. He's Christie.'

Maggie offered her hand and I shook it. The squirrel shot out of my sleeve and ran up her arm, but she didn't take any notice. 'You're a brave boy, to come all this way,' she said.

Danny came next, still covered in birds. They rose like dust as he and Mother embraced and then, like dust, they settled again.

'Are you the brother?' I heard one of them ask him. 'You don't look like the brother. Not very. Are you Colin's brother?'

Tony was steaming like an overheated engine, but Mother passed him and went to greet Tina.

'How wonderful,' she said again, and again the chorus swelled after her. She turned to Tina, who was descending gingerly from the trap, trying not to stand on the scuttling creatures which surrounded her.

'And you are . . .?'

'Stark raving mad, to come to a place like this,' said Tina.

'It's quite possible,' said Mother. 'But you're welcome anyway. Albert said there were three of you, but I thought his sums must be wrong. I'm so glad to see a girl!'

But Tony had waited long enough. 'Stop waffling, Mother,' he said. 'Get this clobber off me!'

She did. I could hear Danny laughing behind me as the pony shook himself hard and rolled in the snow, threatening to flatten some of the smaller animals. I heard the outraged squeals and grunts, but I didn't see the havoc.

Something else had caught my attention. I was looking over at the huge façade of the house, and wondering whether it was an old building or a new one built in traditional style, when I spotted someone who was clearly reluctant to come and join the welcoming throng. Beside the door a small, thin figure crouched against the wall. It could only be Sprog.

Maggie took me by the arm.

'Come on in,' she said. 'You must be worn out.'

There was something strange about the girl, and I turned back to get a better look. But the front of the house was blank. She had already gone.

two

I didn't see her inside, either, and when I asked about her, Maggie said that she was shy, and would turn up when she was ready. I succeeded in staying awake over breakfast, which we ate in the cavernous kitchen at the back of the house. To my disappointment, Maggie ordered all the animals outside, except for the dogs, who were always allowed in, and Darling, whose success in her mission gave her special privileges.

'Just because they can talk doesn't mean they're people,' she told us. 'We don't want them getting soft and spoilt.'

I wanted to hear more, but my exhaustion overcame me. Maggie showed us all upstairs to where seven or eight bedrooms opened off a maze of corridors and landings. When we had seen them all, Maggie told us we could take our pick. I chose the one that was nearest.

In the enormous double bed I slept right around the clock, waking only once to sleep-walk my way to the bathroom.

When I was finally ready to get up, it was around midday, and the whole of that huge house seemed to be empty. I wandered through the silent rooms, hoping to find someone; hoping as well that I might, accidentally-on-purpose, stumble across the lab.

But I didn't find anyone or anything. Even the kitchen was empty; the bare wooden table cleared and scrubbed. The idea came to me that everyone had gone; moved on, or been kidnapped, and a momentary panic erupted from my solar plexus and shot through my limbs. Then, out of the corner of my eye, I caught sight of Sprog.

It was only a glimpse, but it was enough. She had been at the kitchen door, watching me, and had slipped back into the shadows as I turned. I looked up and down the hallway and behind the enormous umbrella plant that stood beside the front door, but I couldn't see her.

'Sprog?' I called.

'Don't call me that,' she said, emerging from the drawing room behind me.

'Sorry,' I said. 'I thought it was your name.'

'Well it's not,' she said, firmly. 'My name is Sandra. You can call me Sandy if you want.'

'OK,' I said. But I wasn't really thinking about what she was saying. I was too busy trying to get a good look at her without appearing to be as gobsmacked as I was. Because she was one of the weirdest people I've ever seen. She was even thinner than Tina, with long, spindly arms and legs, like a stick insect. She had bony hands, with round, prominent knuckles, and her feet seemed far too big for the rest of her; almost clownish. And her face . . .

I dropped my eyes, aware that I was ogling. But it was already imprinted on my mind. Her face was like one of those mummies that you sometimes see pictures of. The skin was brownish, and stretched so tightly over her bones that I could see the shape of her skull beneath.

I didn't succeed in hiding my shock, because she said, defensively, 'I'm one of you.'

I didn't understand. 'Oh?' I said.

'I'm not one of those smart animals. I'm one of you. Like Danny. I'm Danny's sister, you know.'

'Oh,' I said again.

'Half-sister, actually. I don't like it when the animals call me Sprog. Because I'm not.'

I didn't have a clue what she was talking about, but I didn't want to say 'Oh' again. So I said, 'Fine. Pleased to meet you, Sandy.'

She grinned with unexpected delight and her defensiveness evaporated. 'Pleased to meet you, too, Christie. Come on. I've been ordered to give you the grand tour.'

Sandy took a bunch of keys from a hook beside the back door and led the way outside. Oggy and Itchy were lying beneath a bare elder bush chewing on mutton bones, and I wondered briefly if there was ever going to be an end to that old sheep. They abandoned them and joined us, and Sandy unlocked the door of the garage beside the house. Inside was a small BMW, surrounded by mountains of household junk. There were dusty trunks, bits of garden furniture, a shelf of power tools, and boxes of screws and nails.

'Just in case you ever need to fix anything,' said Sandy.

'Nice car,' I said.

'We never use it. Hardly ever, anyway. Sometimes Mother has to drive across the country to get supplies and equipment or seeds.'

'She needs stuff for the lab, I suppose?' I said.

Sandy looked askance at me, and didn't reply.

'Where is it?' I went on. 'The lab, I mean.'

'Out of bounds,' said Oggy.

'No exceptions,' said Itchy.

'Completely forbidden,' said Sandy.

I was disappointed. I wanted to see what a modern lab really looked like, and what went on there. And I wanted to know what Maggie was doing.

'Why is it out of bounds?' I asked.

But if any of them knew, they weren't going to tell me.

three

We closed the garage door behind us and followed a well-trodden pathway in the snow until we came to a fork. One way led towards a smart courtyard surrounded by cut-stone buildings and the other vanished into the shadows of an avenue of tall trees.

I saw Tina walking across the courtyard with a bowl in her hand, and I called out to her. She called back and waved in a cheerful fashion which didn't seem like her at all. I started out along that path, but Sandy said we'd go there on the way back, and led the way with light, springy strides between the trees. Before long we came out of the avenue into a large, bare orchard. Darling was there, rooting for grubs in the withered grass beneath the snow. She was with two of her brothers and a pair of blackbirds, who flew yickering away in panic when we arrived, then returned to natter and cluck from the branches a few yards away.

'Is that all you have to say?' said Sandy.

'Ah, naff off, Sprog.'

I wasn't looking. The three starlings had got mixed up and I was trying to work out which one was Darling. All I heard was a foreshortened rattle of alarm, and when I turned to look, Sandy was standing several metres away with the furious blackbird in her bony hand.

She couldn't have been there. No one could move that fast. My senses were playing tricks on me, some-how.

'My name is Sandy,' she was saying, sternly. 'What's my name?'

'Sandy!' piped the blackbird in strangled tones.

'Again?'

'Sandy, Sandy, Sandy!' said the blackbird.

'And don't forget it!' said Sandy, launching the bird into the high air, where it hung for a moment before diving for cover in a dense bramble thicket.

'Apples,' said Oggy.

'Huh?'

'Apples, pears, plums, cherries. Hardy varieties,' said Sandy. 'Sometimes they even have a bit of fruit on them. Which the birds always get before we do.'

'You should get up earlier,' said Darling.

But my thoughts were elsewhere. 'How did you catch that bird, Sandy?' I asked.

She made a grabbing motion in the air with her long hand but it was meaningless. I had enough on my plate with the talking animals; I couldn't handle any more mysteries just now. It was easier to believe that my perceptions were faulty.

So that was what I did.

four

Beyond the orchards, in a south-facing hollow sheltered on two sides by the hills, was a double row of perspex buildings reflecting the white sky. When I first saw them I thought that they had to be something spectacularly space-age. I was sure that the lab was there, and maybe more; an electronics factory or a communications centre or a space programme. But they were hothouses, that was all. For growing Fourth World's food.

Danny was there with his mother. They were planting out seedlings from trays into a newly-dug bed. When Danny saw me he came trundling over, grabbing a spade on his way.

'Digging, Crumbly,' he said, shoving the spade into the soft earth with characteristic vigour. 'Dig, dig, dig. I digged all that!'

'Good for you, Danny,' I said.

'And now I'm planting. Look, Crinkly, look!'

He did his wobbly dance again, back to Maggie's side and, with his big, clumsy fingers, removed a delicate seedling from the blocking tray, roots, soil and all. Choosing the spot carefully, he set the seedling into the earth and gently firmed it in.

Oggy sniffed at it approvingly.

'It'll grow,' said Danny. 'It'll be a big cabbage for our dinner. They all will.'

He indicated several neat rows of plants that he and Maggie had already put in. Darling and the other birds were hopping between them probing the soft soil with their beaks, and flitting off with worms and grubs.

'Great to get some help at last,' said Maggie. 'It's been quite a struggle since Bernard and Colin left.'

'It has, that,' said Sandy; a bit sourly, I thought.

'Who's Bernard?' I asked.

Sandy said, 'My father,' and Maggie said, 'My partner,' both at the same time. A slight unease entered my heart from somewhere, but I didn't have time to examine it.

'You dig,' said Danny, thrusting the handle of the shovel into my hand. It was the last thing I felt like doing.

'I . . . well . . .' I began.

Maggie laughed. 'No need,' she said. 'We're almost finished here now.'

'No,' said Danny. 'Not finished.'

'You stay, then,' said Maggie. 'Do some more digging. The rest of us are going in for some lunch.'

Danny dropped the shovel as if it was red hot and made

for the door, the little flock of birds scattering ahead of him. The rest of us followed, more slowly.

Maggie fell in beside me. I was flattered and anxious, both at the same time.

'You all right, Christie?' she asked.

'Yeah,' I said. 'Fine.' I prayed that I wasn't blushing. I felt I might be.

'Good,' said Maggie. 'And Danny seems very happy.'

'Danny's always happy,' I said. But I knew what she meant. There was something different about him. As though he belonged here in this off-beat place in a way he had never really belonged out there. In normal society.

We were walking through the snowy orchard. Ahead of me were three of the most unusual people in the world, two unusual dogs, and a flock of unusual birds which, I noticed, seemed to be growing larger. It wasn't only Danny who didn't fit in with regular society. None of them did, and nor, I realised, did Tina. I didn't know how it had come about, but she was already side-lined by the established community. People like her were considered to be failures or drop-outs; embarrassments to be avoided by the great shopping majority.

I dropped behind the others as we walked back, thinking about that 'normal' society, which wasn't so normal any more. I thought about Mom and Maurice and what might be happening at home. I could still hear that answer-phone talking into space, and now I could hear the click as my receiver went down. I wished I had said something. I wished I could talk to Mom now.

But what would I say?

Maybe it was right that I had brought Danny and Tina here, where they could be accepted for what they were. But one big question remained unanswered. What about me?

five

Tina joined us for lunch. She was wearing a pair of clean jeans and a red sweatshirt, presumably on loan from Sandy. There was a spring in her step, and as she sat down at the table I realised, with something resembling a pang of envy, that she, too, seemed to be radiating contentment.

'The goat kids know nearly as much as I do,' she said to Maggie. 'But there's no talk out of the pups yet. I think they're still too young. They keep going to sleep.'

'Pups?' I said.

'I'll take you to see them when we're finished,' said Tina. 'They're absolutely gorgeous! Teeny, tiny Dobermans, all round and podgy.'

'You want to watch their mother,' said Sandy. 'Don't go in on your own until she knows you.'

'Watch their father and their uncle, too,' said Oggy from under the table. 'Grrr. Nasty on a dark night.'

'He's right,' said Maggie. 'And none of them are talking dogs, so there's no point in trying to reason with them. But they'll all be fine when they know you. As soon as they realise you're part of the family.'

I spoke without thinking. 'I'm not part of the family. My family lives in Cork.'

An uncomfortable silence threatened to fall, and Maggie nipped it in the bud. 'Of course,' she said. 'Of course they do. And you're free to go back there any time you want to.'

I knew I wasn't, though. Not while the oil crisis lasted.

'Can I use the phone? Ring Mom?'

'We don't have one,' said Sandy. 'Who would we ever want to talk to?'

'What about your dad?' I said. 'Where has he gone?'

'That's a big story, Christie,' said Maggie. 'We won't go into that now. But we have an Internet connection. Do your folks have e-mail?'

There had been a lot of talk about it, but they never got round to it.

'How can you have the Internet without a phone?' I asked.

'We just don't have a receiver. Decided against it.'

'Why?'

Maggie avoided the question. 'There's a public phone in the village,' she said. 'Oggy will take you, won't you, Oggy?'

'I'll take you,' said Sandy, glaring defiantly at her mother.

'You know that isn't possible, Sandy,' said Maggie, sternly. 'Oggy will take him.'

Oggy was keen to go straight away, but I found I wasn't ready, yet. There was a bone-deep tiredness in my limbs, and I didn't feel like making a snowplough of myself down along the white glen. Instead I went out with Tina to meet what she referred to as 'her babies'.

The goat kid that had nearly strangled me with my scarf was out in the yard with his twin sister. They were bursting with life and stood up against Tina like dogs, begging to be taken for a walk. Tina promised to take them later, but they didn't back off, and tried to follow us in through the door of Iggy's shed.

Tina succeeded in keeping them out, but we could hear them complaining loudly in the courtyard for several minutes afterwards.

When my eyes grew accustomed to the dim light inside, I saw the piglets. They were brand new; hot-pink and wriggly as worms against their mother's long belly.

'Iggy, this is Christie,' said Tina.

'Pleased to meet you,' said Iggy, in long-suffering tones. 'I've been looking forward to it.'

'Oh,' I said, a little taken aback. 'I've been looking forward to it, too.'

'You know I was the first, then,' said Iggy.

'Oh. Well . . .'

'The first talking animal to be born at Fourth World,' said Tina.

'The first ever,' said Iggy, pompously. 'And now I'm the first again. As long as these little milkbags make it.'

'Make what?'

'I'm the first to have my own babies.'

'Mother hopes they'll talk as well,' said Tina.

'Oh, they'll talk,' said Iggy. 'I'm sure of it.'

She sighed hugely and dropped her head on to the clean, yellow straw. 'You'll have to excuse me,' she went on. 'This business really takes it out of you.'

We left her to rest and went to visit the pups. Their mother, Sparky, growled ferociously at me until Tina managed to persuade her that I was OK. After that she was quite content, and didn't seem to mind what we did with her pups.

They were as round and podgy as Tina had said, with squished-up faces and rolls of spare skin all over the place. They weren't really walking, yet, but when we sat down beside them, one of them wriggled her way over to me and tried to wrestle with my fingers.

I picked her up and held her on a level with my eyes. She wagged her stumpy tail so hard that her whole body wagged with it, and her myopic brown eyes were full of smiles.

'Hello,' I said.

' 'Lo,' said the pup.

'She said "hello"!' I cried.

'No she didn't,' said Tina. 'She just squeaked.'

'She didn't,' I said. 'Say it again, pup! Say "hello, Christie".'

The pup made a mewling sound, more like a cat than a dog.

'Hello, Christie,' I said again. And this time there was no mistaking her response.

' 'Lo Ki.'

'Loki!' I laughed, and so did Tina. 'Loki,' I said. 'Loki, Loki, Loki. That's what I'm going to call you.'

We spent a few fruitless minutes trying to get her to repeat it, but her attention had already run out and she was getting dozy. I snuggled her into my lap and stroked her tiny ears as she drifted off, visiting the great unknown she had so recently come from. And, in respect of that awesome place, Tina and I sat quietly and listened to the drip, drip, drip of snow-melt falling from the gutters.

seven

Loki woke up and mewled again, and I put her back with her brothers and sisters. Her nose was a bit more pointed than the others' were, and she had more brown around her eyes. I was sure I'd remember her.

'What do you know about the lab?' I asked Tina.

She shrugged. 'Nothing.'

'You haven't seen it?'

'No. Have you?'

'No. Sandy says it's out of bounds. But I want to.'

'Ask Mother. She might show you.'

I was suddenly irritated. 'Her name is Maggie,' I said. 'Not Mother.'

Tina let it go. 'Why do you want to see it, anyway?' she asked.

'I don't know. Science was the only subject I ever liked in school. I used to think I'd like to be a scientist.'

'I never wanted to be anything,' said Tina. 'Just me.'

The pups were squabbling for position at their mother's milk bar. I made sure Loki got a good position in the fray.

'How come the pups are going to be able to speak when their mother can't?' I said.

Tina stroked the bitch's black head. 'I suppose if you start teaching them when they're young enough . . .'

'No.' I shook my head. 'Loads of people talk to animals. I've got an aunt down the country who has eighteen cats. She's nuts about them. Talks to them all the time, especially the kittens. "Woodgy, woodgy, woodgy, who's my little popsy, then? Does 'oo want milkies?" They never say a thing except miaow. Not a single word.'

'What, then?' said Tina.

'I don't know,' I said. 'It has to be something to do with the lab. Maybe there's some chemical she gives them or something?'

'I don't think she gives them any chemicals,' said Tina. 'She's put me in charge of all the feeding and there isn't anything in the food.'

'How do you know? Maybe it's already in it?'

Tina shook her head. 'Anyway, all the babies are feeding from their mothers, so they couldn't be getting it, could they?'

'Maybe she's giving them drops, or injections or something. When you're not looking.'

Loki unlatched herself from her mother and began to squirm away. Not towards Tina, or the door, or anything else. Towards me. I felt absurdly flattered, and picked her up again.

222

'Loki?' I said. 'Loki?'

I hugged her against my neck and she licked me with a tiny, wet tongue.

'I bet it's something like that,' I said. 'It has to be. Do you think Maggie would let me see where the lab is?'

'Why don't you ask her?' Tina picked up another of the pups. 'Say hello,' she pleaded. 'Hello.'

But the pup just wuffled breathlessly, and tried to bite her fingers.

eight

There were other animals to see, but now that I was on track of a mystery I couldn't let it go. I went back to the house and, finding it empty, searched it from top to bottom. But there was no lab, no locked door, no clues.

I wandered outside again and followed the slushy path to the hothouses. Danny was there, singing and digging. Oggy and Itchy were lounging in the warmth, watching.

'Hi, Danny.'

'Hi, Kissy-face.'

Still Danny, but definitely different. As I watched him work, I wondered whether Maurice had been mistaken all along, keeping him at home and confined. Maybe all Danny had ever needed was something he could do; some purpose to his life; some outlet for his phenomenal energy. He was focused now in a way that I had never seen before, and I was reminded of the words that he had spoken to me that day in Inverness.

'Mother's going to show me what I am.'

'Want to dig?' he said now.

'No thanks, Danny. I'm looking for Maggie.'

'She's in the lavatory,' he said.

'Laboratory,' said Itchy.

'Where is it?' I asked.

The dogs got shifty and wouldn't look at me.

'Three old ladies locked in the laboratory,' sang Danny.

'All right,' I said. 'Be like that. Where's Sandy?'

'Dam,' said Itchy.

'No need to swear,' I said.

'No, no,' said Oggy. 'She's at the dam. I'll take you there.'

As we walked up the hillside, some of Fourth World's wilder residents came out of the woods and the heather to meet us. A squirrel that I thought I recognised, and a pair of rabbits that sat on their hind legs and seemed to be whispering together. They answered me when I called softly to them, but they kept their distance and didn't join us.

The dam looked more like a small lake to me, but Sandy assured me it had been man-made; built to collect the water from two strong streams that ran down the hillsides. She was probing beneath the dark water with a long pole as she spoke.

'Ice in the sluicegate.'

She lifted the pole and plunged it down against the

unseen blockage. I suppose it must have been not work, because her jacket and sweatshirt were slung across a nearby bush, and she was down to her t-shirt. The muscles on her thin arms were so prominent and clearly defined that it was like looking at an anatomical drawing.

I dragged my gaze away from them.

'Why do you need to clear it?' I asked.

'No wind,' she said. 'And not much sun.'

'Eh?'

'It's where we get our power from, brain-box.' She slammed down on the pole with a strength that surprised me. 'We have a water-driven generator.'

'Oh,' I said.

The two rabbits had followed behind us and suddenly Oggy woofed and tore off after them. I thought he was serious and that they were in trouble, but a few moments later I realised it was a game; they were all racing in circles in the slushy heather, having a ball.

Sandy gave another mighty heave on the pole. There was a slurp and a gurgle from somewhere below, and then the sound of water running freely through a large pipe.

'Hooray!' said Sandy.

She pulled out the pole and laid it down under the cover of the bushes, then pulled on her sweater and jacket. Her mood had clearly improved.

'We have wind turbines as well, over there.'

I hadn't noticed them on the way up, but they were clearly visible now, turning very slowly on the brow of one of the hills.

'And solar panels on the house and sheds. See?'

The whole of Fourth World was spread out below us; the house and buildings, the orchards and hothouses and beyond, another row of buildings that I hadn't seen before, standing among a range of neatly fenced fields. I asked Sandy what they were, and was disappointed by her reply.

'Farm buildings. Cow-shed, chicken house, granary, hay-barn.'

'Where's the lab, then?' I asked, trying to sound innocent.

'The lab,' said Sandy, 'is no one's business except Mother's.'

'Have you been in it?'

'No. I've never set foot in it, not since the day I was born.'

'But why?' I said. 'Why does it have to be so secret?'

'If you don't know the answer to that,' said Sandy, snidely, 'you're a bigger fool than you look.'

On the way down the hillside Sandy stopped in a sheltered hollow where several tall ash trees had been spared by the wind.

'Can you climb trees?' she said.

'Yes. Of course,' I said. I wasn't sure that it was true. I hadn't climbed a tree since I was about nine.

Sandy pointed to the tallest one. 'Bet I could get to the top before you.'

I didn't accept the challenge. My energy hadn't returned yet, and besides, I didn't feel that I had anything to prove.

'I'm sure you could,' I said, and walked on down towards the house.

nine

That evening we had a dinner of eggs in cheese sauce with potatoes and broccoli. I watched Maggie as she served it up, wondering where she got her energy from, and what it was about her that made me feel so self-conscious when she was around. I knew that she liked me; she always had a kind word or a smile. And I found as I watched her that I couldn't believe she was doing anything wrong here in Fourth World. Nothing bad, at least.

Danny ate mountains of food, ravenous after all his digging. He had entirely finished one of the glasshouses and had made good inroads on a second.

'You can dig in the outside garden as soon as the snow clears,' Maggie told him. 'Get it ready for planting the potatoes.'

'Potatoes,' said Danny, his mouth full of them. 'Growing potatoes.'

For a while we all concentrated on our plates. I don't know what was in anyone else's mind, but I was still thinking about Maggie and her mysteries. She glanced across at me and winked. I looked away, trying to hide the blush that I knew was rising to my cheeks. As I did so, I realised that one of the things I liked about her was that she didn't treat us like children. Never had. I remembered the book she had brought for me. *Catastrophe Theory*. That wasn't a kids' book. It was a respectful present to an equal.

That was what decided me.

'Can I see the lab, Maggie?'

Just for a split second, I thought I saw an expression of fear in her eyes. Then it was gone, and the light with it, as though she had turned herself off inside.

'The lab is out of bounds,' she said.

'But I wouldn't touch anything. I just want to see.'

'End of conversation,' said Maggie.

I put down my knife and fork, fuming, unable to believe what I had been telling myself just a few minutes before. That intimate manner was just a trick. Her own way of trying to win us over, that was all.

For a few minutes I succeeded in pulling the mood of the table down to the level of my sulk. Then Tina broke free.

'One of the pups spoke to Christie today,' she said.

'Really?' said Maggie. 'What did it say?'

Tina looked at me but I didn't answer. 'Loki,' she said. 'We think. Christie is going to call her Loki.'

'Good name,' said Maggie, trying to engage me. But I looked away, and the conversation went on without me. Soon afterwards Sandy cleared away my unfinished meal, and Maggie produced a big jug of cream and a bowl of raspberries.

'Frozen,' she said. 'But still good.'

After the hungry weeks on the road, those raspberries were the most tempting thing I had ever seen. But I was still under protest.

'No thanks,' I said, and left the table.

I went outside into the yard and Oggy slipped out behind me. The dripping of the thaw had stopped, and everything was freezing hard again. Above us the stars were bright and cold.

I had left the house with the intention of going to the phone box in the village, but now that I was out there it seemed too dark, too cold, too far.

Oggy stayed quiet, as though the world felt too big for him, too, and after a while we went back inside.

But I didn't rejoin the others, even though their cheerful chat coming from the kitchen was exactly the warmth I needed just then. Instead I made my way upstairs and got into bed.

I don't know how long I stayed awake. I heard Maggie helping Danny to bed next door, both of them laughing. A little later Tina and Sandy came up, and soon after that the moon rose and crept into the edge of my window frame. I was still awake when it completed its shallow arc and inched out at the other side.

There were too many things unexplained. What was Maggie giving to the animals to enable them to speak? And why was it such a secret? What was wrong with Sandy that made her look so strange? And why was no one willing to talk about her father and where he had gone to?

And hadn't there been mention of someone called Colin? Where did he fit in?

I couldn't think of any sinister implications in the mysteries of Fourth World, but the secrecy which surrounded everything made me suspicious. If someone took the trouble to explain things to me, I could make up my own mind about the rights and wrongs of the place. But they didn't, so I couldn't.

Tomorrow I would definitely phone home and tell them what was happening. Maybe Maurice would cast some light on things. He had lived here, after all. Even if it was a long time ago.

But thoughts of Maurice created more anxiety than they cured. If he knew Danny was here he would probably insist on taking him away again. There might be more arguments, like the one that had happened in our house. Could I let all that happen?

One thing, and one thing alone, I was certain about. No matter how off-beam Fourth World might appear, Danny belonged here. Did I really want to get him taken away?

It could be worse. Maurice might blow the whistle on

Maggie, and the Law might become involved. But why? For what?

I had arrived back at the beginning and my mind set out on the familiar, fruitless course all over again. I knew there was no more point to it, but I didn't know how to stop. I was still thinking, and it was well into the small hours when I felt the movement of minuscule feet on my sheets, and the weight of a tiny warmth snuggling up to my chin.

I caught it in my hand and reached for the bedside light.

'Oh, blast it,' said the pink mouse, blinking at the sudden light. 'I thought you were asleep!'

'And I thought you were supposed to be outside!' I said, trying to sound more stern than I felt.

'I'm a mouse!' he said, indignantly. 'Since when did mice ask permission to live in people's houses?'

I laughed and switched off the lamp. And with the tiny creature snuggled in the hollow of my collar bone, I slept like a log until daybreak.

ten

The next morning brought no new insights. It did bring news of the outside world, though.

'Private cars have been banned from the roads,' said Maggie, over breakfast. 'Except for the emergency services. And the army is taking over public transport. No one's allowed to travel without applying for permission.'

I wondered if I would get permission. If I threw myself upon the mercy of the army, would they get me home to Ireland? I doubted it, somehow.

'Bicycles are in great demand,' Maggie went on. 'Can't be had for love nor money. The delivery boy is back on the road again. They can't get enough of them.'

'Will they be able to make it out here?' I asked.

'What for?' said Sandy. 'Everything we eat, we grow.'

As soon as breakfast was over, Danny scooted off to the greenhouses with Maggie, and Tina went out to care for her tiny friends. I was mooching around, thinking about the phones again, when Sandy asked me for help in the chicken house.

The snow had a new, crisp coating of ice on the top, but already the day was warming up and beginning to soften it.

'Any chance you'd answer a few of my questions?' I asked Sandy, cautiously.

'You never know,' she said. 'Ask away.'

'How come the animals talk?'

'Just making conversation, I suppose.'

'Ha, ha,' I said. 'You know what I meant.'

'Ask Mother,' said Sandy.

'Oh, good idea,' I said, with heavy sarcasm. 'She's sure to tell me. While she's giving me the grand tour of the lab.'

'I tell you what,' said Sandy, suddenly brightening. 'I'll make a deal with you, OK?'

The approach to the farm buildings took us along an avenue of tall, Scots pines. 'If you can beat me to the top of one of these trees,' said Sandy, 'I'll tell you anything you want to know. How's that for an offer?'

It sounded fair. 'What is it with you and trees?' I asked.

Sandy smiled. 'I'm good at getting up high.'

But it was still worth a try. I had nothing to lose, after all. 'Which tree?' I said.

'You choose. Any one you like.'

I pointed out a strong one whose lowest branches were within reach. Then Sandy said, 'Ready, steady . . . Go!'

I sprinted across the gravel and leapt for the first branch, realising as I did so that my desire for knowledge was strong enough to give me an extra bit of impulsion. My speed seemed to have left Sandy for dead; I couldn't hear her behind me as I clambered up, hand over hand. But about halfway up the trunk I came to a sticky spot and had to stop. There was a bare patch where a branch had broken, and there were no footholds. I was going to have to reach high and walk myself up. If I dared.

I still couldn't hear Sandy, and glanced back to see how much of a start I had. She was nowhere to be seen. In sudden confusion, I peered around to the other side of the trunk and scanned the ground, already far below. There was no sign of her at all.

I experienced a sinking feeling, wondering if she was making a fool of me; sending me shinning up a tree that she had no intention of climbing herself. Then, without warning, I heard a clatter and crackle of branches high above my head. I ducked involuntarily, and clung to the trunk to get my balance.

Then I looked up.

Sandy was sitting in the tree-top, perching on a cluster of thin, springy branches that seemed far too flimsy to bear the weight of a human being. I looked down again. She hadn't set out ahead of me, and I was certain that she hadn't overtaken me. It was impossible that she should be up there. But she was.

'How did you do that?' I said.

She grinned down at me, her eyes bright with mischief.

'Can't tell you,' she said. 'You didn't win, so you don't get any answers.'

I must have spent twenty minutes investigating that tree and the others around it. I knew there had to be a rope somewhere; a sling or a pulley or a slide. But I didn't find anything that could explain how Sandy got up there.

And while I was looking, Sandy got to do the nicer of the two jobs that were waiting for us at the henhouse, which was collecting the eggs.

The other job, which I had to share with her, was torture. For the rest of the morning we scraped and shovelled and barrowed the stinking droppings from the henhouse floor and dumped them on to a muck-heap at the side. I suppose I must have done a lot of complaining, because at one stage Sandy put down her shovel and snapped, 'I wish you'd stop moaning! I milked the cows and fed the hens and put the goats out on the mountain before you even got up this morning!'

I did stop moaning, but I didn't stop thinking. And I discovered, for the first time, that sometimes hard work can free up your mind, even while it ties up your body. Because things began to shift and settle in my head. Not much, but a bit.

The first thing that happened was that, after Sandy reminded me how hard she worked, that uneasy feeling returned. Only this time it was worse; more demanding.

237

What was it that Maggie had said in the hothouse that time?

'It's been quite a struggle since Bernard and Colin left.'

A small area of the vast darkness was illuminated for me. One question, at least, had been answered. I remembered Tina asking what kind of a woman was it who would send for her son after fifteen years. Now I knew.

A woman who needed a labour force.

I nearly threw down my shovel there and then, but something made me carry on. Now that my thoughts had begun to lead somewhere I didn't want to cut them off prematurely. So I worked on and, although I was practically shoulder to shoulder with Sandy, I wasn't really there at all. We worked in silence, each of us in a world of our own.

By the time we had finished the job I had done an awful lot of thinking. I hadn't come up with any more insights, but I had made a few resolutions. The first was that I was going to keep on asking questions until I got some answers. The second was that I wasn't going to give Maggie the satisfaction of becoming her slave. Somehow, some time, I was going to go home. But not, I promised myself, until I had carried out my third resolution. No matter what it took, I was going to get inside that lab.

part
nine

one

There were oatcakes and cheese and some sort of dark, stringy salad greens for lunch. I started with the questions straight away.

'So where has the mysterious Bernard disappeared to?'

Sandy spluttered green debris across the scrubbed boards of the table.

'Mysterious?' she gasped, puce with laughter. 'Dad?'

'Oh, I don't know,' said Maggie. 'I sometimes felt he was a bit of a mystery.'

'Not to me, he isn't!' said Sandy, collecting the scattered bits of her mouthful. 'I can read him like a book.'

'Well, anyway,' I said, trying to restore order. 'Mysterious or not, where is he?'

'Africa, we think,' said Maggie. She gestured towards an untidy heap of letters on one of the worktops, pinned against the wall by a large turnip. 'At least, they were when we last heard from them. But now that the post has gone haywire there's no way of knowing. They could be anywhere.'

Sandy went quiet and I wondered if she was missing them.

'What are they doing in Africa?' said Tina.

'Research,' said Maggie.

'Are they part of an expedition?' I asked, picturing a line of men in bush shorts and *sola topis* sweating their way into the interior.

Maggie shook her head. 'Just the two of them. Bernard and Colin. And a few of the animals. It's to do with a little project we've been working on together.'

Sandy was still quiet.

'Is Colin your brother?' I asked her.

She gave me a swift, hostile look. 'The biggest pest under the sun,' she said. 'Daddy's little favourite.'

Maggie looked uncomfortable.

'What was the project?' I asked her.

'Oh, nothing terribly interesting. It's to do with fossils. Remains of prehistoric man.'

'Prehistoric man?' I said. 'Not interesting?'

Maggie laughed. 'You like that kind of thing?'

'I love it,' I said, truthfully. 'All those discoveries. Bits of skulls and stuff.'

'Those are just the high points,' said Maggie. 'The bits that make the headlines. I'm afraid the everyday nitty gritty is nothing like that at all.'

'What is it like, then?'

'Oh, just boring old examination and analysis.'

'All the same,' I said, trying to sound eager and innocent. 'I'd love to know how you do it.'

I thought I was getting somewhere; coming close to winning her over, but Danny threw a spanner in the works.

'Finished, Mother. Digging some more?'

'You'll break your back, young man,' she said. 'Why don't you take a break from digging?'

Danny looked disappointed, but Maggie went on, 'How about sowing some seeds instead? It's time the broad beans went in. Sandy'll show you how, won't you, Sandy?'

'Thanks, Mother,' said Sandy.

'Thanks, Mother,' echoed Danny, but without the sarcastic undertone.

'Why don't *you* show him?' asked Sandy

'I have things that need attending to.'

My ears pricked up. I was sure she was going to work in the lab. I waited until Sandy and Danny left, and then I helped clear away the breakfast things. I stayed close to Mother, knowing I was going to suck up to her; not caring if it got me what I wanted.

When Tina left, I said, 'What's eating Sandy?'

Maggie sighed. 'She wanted to go with Bernard. She thought it wasn't fair that Colin went instead of her. He's younger, you know. Only nine.' She looked as though it hurt, having him so far away from her.

'And why did Bernard take him instead of Sandy?'

'He . . . well . . .' She stopped and looked hard at me. 'You can see for yourself, can't you?'

She was beginning to distance herself.

'It's because she looks odd, isn't it?'

Maggie nodded.

'And that's why you don't let her go to the village, isn't it?'

Again Maggie nodded, and for a moment I felt her heart was beginning to go out to me; that she needed to confide. 'Why does she look so strange?' I asked, softly.

But Maggie saw through me, and smiled a sly smile. 'Who knows?' she said.

You do, I thought, but I didn't say it. I got the brush and scrubbed the table industriously, then said, as nonchalantly as I could, 'Anything I can help you with?'

'No, Christie,' she said. 'Thanks all the same.'

She went upstairs, and I hovered around in the kitchen until I realised that it was going to look pretty obvious if I tried to follow her when she came down. So I went out to Tina and the animals.

She was in with the piglets. I fought off the goat kids and went in with her, but I stayed beside the door, from where I had a good view of the back of the house.

Tina was making *oochy-koochy* noises to the piglets. 'Mother says I should stimulate them early,' she said. 'Get their brains receptive.'

244

'Oh yes,' I said.

She continued her mindless babble, and Iggy joined in. That kind of stuff turned my stomach, but I didn't have to put up with it for long. Maggie came out of the back door of the house and walked along beside the wall. I edged forward, trying to keep her in view. She went into the garage by the small door at the side and closed it behind her. I slipped out of Iggy's shed and crept along the wall of the courtyard, trying to persuade the kids to shut up and leave me alone. By the time I got to the gate, Maggie still hadn't emerged. I slipped through, leaving the kids trying to climb over, and darted across the wet snow to the opposite side of the garage.

I had planned to peep in through the window, but now I realised that there wasn't one. I walked around the building, taking care to be quiet, but there were none on the other sides, either. No windows at all.

It was weird. I had never come across a garage without a window. At the big up-and-over door I stopped and listened for a while, but there was no sound coming from inside.

'Looking for something?'

The voice was right beside me. I nearly jumped out of my skin. But it was only Oggy, who had padded up beside me on silent paws.

'Oh, Oggy,' I said. 'You gave me a fright.'

'You're slinking,' said Oggy. 'Why are you slinking?'

'I'm not slinking,' I said. 'I'm just . . .'

'Just?'

'Just looking for Maggie.'

Oggy listened hard at the door for a moment. Then he said, 'Not in there, anyway.'

'No,' I said. 'I suppose she isn't.'

It shook me, finding myself lying to Oggy. We were friends; we had been through thick and thin together, dependent upon each other for our survival. But here, among the secrets of Fourth World, I was no longer sure that I had any allies.

'Let's go in,' said Oggy. 'Maybe she's just being very quiet?'

I had assumed that the small door must be locked, but it wasn't, and as I eased it open I searched my mind for a reason to be looking for Maggie. Because I knew she was in there. I had seen her go in, just minutes before.

The garage was dark. I switched on the light. There was a momentary pink scurry in the corner as my little mouse friend dived for cover, but there was nothing else moving in there at all.

A chill crept up my back and neck. She had to be here somewhere. I looked inside the car and under it.

'She's not here, Christie,' said Oggy. 'If she was I'd smell her.'

Unless she had crammed herself into one of the old trunks, he had to be right. But it didn't make sense. As we closed the door behind us I stood still and tried to orient myself in a world where people had the power to appear in the tops of trees and disappear from closed buildings. But no matter how hard I tried, I failed.

three

At dinner that night I was still too bewildered to follow up on my questioning campaign. The big mysteries were too scary and couldn't be asked about, and the smaller ones were like minnows swimming among sharks. Instead I listened to Danny warbling on about beans, and Tina giving her baby report, and Maggie and Sandy fielding all the enthusiasm with smug satisfaction.

Tina was the worst. In her new contentment she had somehow become watered down, like the weak coffee Mom used to give me when I was little. There was no edge to her any more. No spirit. She even volunteered to wash up after dinner. I preferred her the way she was before; spikes and all.

I made a few helpful gestures, like putting away the butter, and was about to go to bed and think, when the Dobermans on patrol set up a terrifying din out in the grounds.

Everyone froze. Even Danny.

'It's coming from the hothouses,' said Sandy.

'I think you're right,' said Maggie. 'Let's go and take a look.'

She grabbed a sheep lamp from a charger on the wall, and Sandy shrugged herself into a jacket.

'What's happening?' I said.

'Sounds like visitors,' said Sandy.

'But you can't go out there in the dark,' I said. 'They might be dangerous.'

Sandy laughed. 'We can be pretty dangerous ourselves, you know.'

Danny had turned pale and was beginning to suck air. It was the first time since we had arrived that he'd looked even vaguely unsettled.

'Not now, Danny,' I said, sharply. 'If you don't want to cause trouble, you'd better hold.'

His expression became even more fearful, but he knew it was serious, and he held. Maggie looked at him, then at me, then back to him again. Sandy opened the door, and Oggy and Itchy shot out into the night and were gone.

'Have you got a gun?' said Tina.

'A gun?' said Maggie. 'What would I want with a gun?'

'They might be armed,' said Tina. 'Whoever they are.'

'And would there be fewer deaths and fewer injuries if we all were?' said Maggie.

But her words cut no ice with Tina. She was pale and trembling, and despite the gravity of the situation I had time to be surprised. In all the weeks I'd known Tina she had never shown the slightest hint of fear. She hadn't even put any value on her own life. But this new change that had come over her seemed even more profound than I had imagined.

Then, suddenly, I understood. For the first time in her life, Tina had a home. Not only a home, but a calling: her young animals, her little dependents. She had found something worth living for, and now she was terrified of losing it.

Sandy was standing in the open doorway, letting in the freezing night air.

'Come on, Mother,' she said.

On the other side of the orchard, Oggy and Itchy had joined in the frenzied barking. But Maggie was still staring at Danny, who was continuing to hold his breath. Maggie turned to me.

'Do you know how long he can do that for?' she asked.

'Oh, ages,' I said. 'Ages and ages.'

'How long?'

'Seven minutes. Maybe more.'

Despite the unknown menace waiting in the darkness, Maggie smiled; a broad grin of delighted satisfaction.

'I knew it,' she said, softly. 'I knew it.'

four

Then she was gone, and Sandy as well, out into the night. I was scared witless, but I had to go. Not because I wanted to, but because staying and not knowing would be worse.

'No, Christie,' said Tina, as I grabbed my jacket. 'Not you as well!'

So she did care about me. It gave me courage.

'You're not going, Christie. You hear me?'

It was a bit more like the old Tina. I knew that if I stayed another moment she would succeed in getting her own way.

'Look after Danny!' I said, and pelted off across the snow after the bouncing beam of the lamp.

There were three men pinned against the outer wall of the greenhouses. They had long sticks and had succeeded in keeping the dogs at bay, but they were wise enough to know that they couldn't run.

'Call them off!' shouted one as we approached.

'What are you doing here?' Maggie called back. There wasn't the slightest fear or doubt in her voice.

'Call off your dogs!'

'Not until we get an explanation.'

We took up position behind the four dogs and shone the lamp on the men. They had a torch as well, but its beam was weak and we knew they couldn't see us as well as we could see them.

'You have all this food,' said the taller of the three. 'We needed a bit to eat for our families.'

'You didn't think to ask?' said Maggie.

Any doubts I had about her dissolved. I was proud just to be there, standing beside her, soaking in her natural authority and fearlessness.

The men were silent. They didn't look like bad guys to me. They looked ordinary, maybe a bit hard up. Like everybody now, I supposed. Everybody except Fourth World.

'They say you're strange folk,' said another man, at last. He had a short beard, as though he had recently stopped bothering to shave.

'We're strange folk, all right,' said Sandy. 'You're better off keeping out of our way.'

'We will, aye,' said the tall man. 'If you just call off your dogs.'

Maggie did.

'Down!'

Just one word, and all four dogs backed off and dropped, panting, at our feet. The men unglued themselves from the wall and moved forward. I thought they'd go, just melt back into the night they had emerged from, but the unshaven man stepped right up to Maggie, undeterred by the growling of the dogs.

'It's no' right,' he said. 'Why should you have all this food when folk out there have none?'

'Because we grew it,' said Sandy. 'That's why.'

The tall man said, 'Come on, boys,' and moved away. But it wasn't over yet. The bearded man said, 'Would you have given it to us if we'd asked?'

Maggie thought for a moment, and then said, 'No. In the summer perhaps, if we had a surplus. But we haven't, now. We have only enough for ourselves.'

The other two men were some distance away already, and they called to their friend again. But he still wasn't ready to join them.

'You snotty cow,' he snarled. 'Standing there all smug with your guff about summer surpluses. I'll give you something surplus all right.'

He swung the heavy stick back, ready to launch a massive blow at Maggie. It seemed to me that nothing could stop him from knocking her brains out, but I was wrong. The pups' father, Obi, was on his feet and ready to spring, but someone else had reacted even faster.

It was Sandy. She had already jumped into the air and,

before the man could start his swing, she lashed out with a karate kick that hit the man plumb in the middle of the chest. The jump and kick were spectacular in themselves, but what was even more amazing was the power behind them. The man's feet left the ground and he flew backwards for a metre or so before he crashed into the snow, flat on his back.

Before his friends could get to him the dogs were up again, forming a bristling cordon between them and us. Maggie waited until the bearded man got up, clutching his chest and gasping. Then she called the dogs off.

'I don't expect to see you here again,' she said, as the two uninjured men helped the other one to shuffle away.

They didn't answer. We stood in the snow and watched them until they were out of sight, and then we turned back, leaving Obi and his brother, Kanobi, to their nocturnal patrolling of Fourth World.

As we walked back towards the house, I fell into step beside Sandy.

'That was pretty impressive,' I said. 'Where did you learn to do that?'

Sandy shrugged and flashed her bright smile. 'It just comes naturally,' she said.

five

That night I lay awake again, and again the moon began to peer around the edge of my window. I was a jumble of emotion, a bit elated, a bit scared, and full of proud admiration for Maggie and for Sandy, who had acted so bravely that night.

But as my excitement began to settle I found that underneath it all, my resolutions were intact. I still wanted answers. I still wanted to go home. I still wanted to get into the lab. More than ever, now.

Maybe Maggie and Sandy had both been invisible for a while? A chemical for becoming invisible and a chemical for making animals talk. It was too far-fetched. But no matter how hard I racked my brains I couldn't come up with anything better. I hoped the little mouse would come again, and sure enough he did, about half an hour later. We chatted for a while and he told me his name was Claus. Then I remembered where it was I had last seen him, and I realised that he might be able to offer more than company.

'Did you see Maggie in the garage today?' I asked.

'Maggie?'

'Mother, I mean,' I said.

' 'Course,' said Claus. 'Two or three times. Saw you and Oggy as well.'

'That's right,' I said. 'But what was Ma . . . Mother doing there?'

'Same as usual,' said Claus. 'Just passing through.'

'Passing through?'

'On her way down below.'

Of course! What better place to conceal a secret building than underneath the ground? I sat up, took Claus gently in my cupped palms, and held him close to my face.

'Can you show me?' I whispered. 'Can you show me how to get down there?'

Claus ruffled his creamy coat and sat up on his haunches. 'What's in it for me?' he asked.

'What do you want?'

He thought for a moment, then said, 'Oats. A few oats left out every night. In the corner behind the barrel. And a little bit of cheese?'

'Done,' I said. 'When can you show me?'

'Anything wrong with now?' said Claus.

'Not a thing,' I said.

six

Claus hung on to my collar as I crept down the stairs, my boots in my hand. At the bottom step I stopped and whispered to him.

'Are Oggy and Itchy in the kitchen?'

'No,' he whispered back. I wouldn't have heard him at all if he hadn't been practically inside my ear. 'They go out at night to help Obi and Kanobi.'

'Good.'

'Why good?'

I shrugged thoughtlessly, tipping Claus upside down so he had to scramble up on to my shoulder again.

'Sorry.'

The kitchen door was locked, but the bunch of keys was hanging on a hook beside it. I took it down and tried each key until I found the right one, then slipped out into the frozen night.

Claus crept under my collar to borrow the heat of my skin. I hadn't turned on any lights or brought the lamp, for fear of giving myself away. Out there in the night, despite the moonlight reflecting from the snow, my skin crawled. There had already been one set of intruders, and I didn't fancy meeting any more. With every nerve-end on red alert, I turned the key in the garage door and went inside.

It was pitch dark in there. I considered going back for the lamp until I remembered that the building had no windows, and that it would be safe to turn on the light. The glare was blinding after the moonlight outside, and for a few moments I had to keep my eyes closed. When I opened them the garage looked as empty and innocent as before. But now I knew that it was deceptive; a cleverly disguised threshold to a hidden, and possibly illegal, world.

I walked all around the car, examining the ground, but I couldn't see anything that looked like a trap door.

'Where is it, Claus?' I asked.

He wriggled out from under my collar and sat up, his whiskers tickling my neck.

'Put me down,' he said. 'I'll show you.'

He ran on ahead to the front of the car and vanished among the clutter of broken deck-chairs and watering cans. When I next caught sight of him he was sitting on top of a large, tin trunk.

'Under here,' he said.

I tried to shift the trunk but it wouldn't budge.

'No, no,' piped Claus. 'Under there!'

He pointed with his nose at a heap of oily rags which lay beside the trunk. They looked as though they had been casually dropped by a mechanic, but when I made to shift them I found that they, like the trunk, were fastened to the floor. Claus dropped down to help, and tugged at a loose corner. I must admit that I had begun to doubt his sanity, but now I saw that he was telling the truth. Beneath the corner of the rag was a Chub lock and an inset handle for lifting the whole section of floor; trunk, rags and all.

'Brilliant!' I said.

There was no Chub key on the bunch in my hand, but it didn't worry me. After all, I knew someone who was a whiz at picking locks.

seven

I slept late after my wakeful night. By the time I came down, Tina and Sandy had already gone off about their business, and only Danny and Maggie were in the kitchen.

'Hi, Danny,' I said. He waved a big, flappy hand but said nothing.

Maggie pointed to a snazzy steel clock on the table that looked as though it might have come out of a lunar module.

'Five minutes and counting,' she said.

I helped myself to gloopy porridge and honey, and sat down to eat it at the table. Maggie never once took her eyes off Danny.

'When you can't hold it any longer,' she said, 'take one big breath and hold it again, will you?'

Danny nodded, happy to please. I gobbled the porridge and went back for more. When Danny finally let his breath out the clock registered seven minutes and thirty-nine seconds. As he drew in another, Maggie reset the clock and settled in to watch him again.

'I think it might be why he's so scatty,' she said. 'He gets too much oxygen to his brain under normal circumstances.'

It made sense. 'He always seems to be clear-headed after he holds his breath,' I said. 'And in the mornings.'

'Does he?' said Maggie. 'That fits.'

'But why?' I asked. 'What would make him like that?'

Maggie shook her head, as though she didn't know. When I finished my breakfast and set out to find Tina, the clock was reading six minutes and forty-three seconds.

Tina was educating some kittens that I hadn't met before, and Itchy was looking on with a benign but shuttered gaze, as though she might change her mind given half an excuse and swallow them all whole. Their mother, perched on the windowsill, watched her like a hawk.

'Paws,' said one kitten.

'Claws,' said another.

'Hello, Christie,' said Tina.

'Hello, Christie,' echoed the kittens.

'Come to help?' said Tina.

I couldn't speak freely in front of Itchy. 'Yeah,' I said, sitting down beside Tina on a straw bale.

The kittens were at their most enchanting age, more interested in playing tiger games than in concentrating on their lessons. But their vocabulary was already impressive and they seemed to pick up new words and phrases without effort, far more quickly, I thought, than human children did.

'They develop much quicker,' said Tina. 'In every way.'

'Develop much quicker,' said one of the kittens.

'In every way,' said another.

Tina gave them a bowl of fresh cream as a reward for their endeavours, and then we left them. In the yard we met Sandy, coming to fetch the kids' mother and take her out to the mountain-side with the other goats.

'How can they graze when there's so much snow?' I asked.

'They browse,' said Sandy. 'Bushes and heather and stuff.'

To my relief, Itchy went with her to help keep the little flock in order, and I was alone with Tina at last. We went into the shed where Sparky lived, and I called to the sleeping muddle of pups.

'Loki?'

One tiny head shot up, and then she was squirming out of the puppy mass and searching the floor for me, her tiny tail going nineteen to the dozen. I picked her up. There was no doubt about it. This one was my dog.

She chewed on my little finger as I spoke to Tina.

'I found out where the lab is.'

'Oh?'

I kept my voice low. 'It's under the garage. There's a trap door.'

'Very clever. Did Mother show you after all?'

'No. A little mouse did.'

'How sweet,' said Tina, with something of her old, familiar cynicism. I ignored it.

'It's locked, though,' I said.

'It would be, I suppose.'

'So I was wondering . . .'

'Yeah?'

'I was wondering if you'd come with me. Tonight, after everyone's in bed. You can open it and we'll sneak in and have a look.'

I really thought she'd be on for it; as curious and enthusiastic as I was. But she thought for a long moment, and then said, 'No.'

'No?' I yelped.

'No. If Mother doesn't want us in there I'm sure she has her reasons.'

I couldn't believe this was Tina sitting beside me, talking like that.

'Oh,' I said, lamely. And then, as my resentment surfaced, 'Now who's Goody-Two-Shoes, then? Eh?'

It just rolled off her.

'This place is different, Christie. This world makes sense to me.'

'Sense?' I said. 'It makes no sense at all, Tina. Not a bit. That's why I want to go into the lab, see? To try and understand what's happening here!'

But Tina had already shut me out. She picked up one of the other pups and looked it in the eye.

'Tina,' she said. 'Say "Tina".'

'Tee,' squeaked the pup.

'Hear that?' said Tina.

I put Loki back with her mum and moved to the door. 'I don't know *what* I'm hearing in here,' I said. 'I can't really believe any of it.'

eight

I mooched around for the rest of the morning, not knowing what to do with myself. I felt like a misfit; completely out of place. Everyone else had a purpose here; something which kept them occupied and motivated. But I was adrift, at odds with everyone and everything, and my only ally in the whole place was a small, pink mouse.

I couldn't bear to be around Tina any more, so I wandered over and helped Danny, who was digging in the outside garden despite the layer of old snow which still covered the ground. Not for the first time, I envied him his simple existence.

'I'm a gardener, Crusty,' he told me, proudly. It was all he wanted. But it wasn't for me. Digging made my back hurt, and it was boring. After a while I left him to it and made my way back to the house. I was in a foul mood, but just as I was nearing the back door I saw something which set my heart racing and filled me with new optimism.

Maggie was emerging from the garage on her way to make lunch. As she closed the door behind her, I saw her drop a single brass Chub key into the pocket of her jacket.

Now I knew where she kept it. Tonight, I would get into the lab.

part
ten

one

I didn't forget my promise to Claus. Before I went to bed I took it upon myself to get the porridge ready for the morning, and made sure to scatter a few oats and a tiny piece of cheese into the dark corner.

Up in my room, I discovered that I was desperate for some sleep, but I stayed awake, listening to every sound in the house. At around midnight, Claus arrived on my pillow, but the lights were still on at the back of the house and I knew that Maggie hadn't gone to bed yet.

I filled Claus in on what I had seen and what I intended to do. If he didn't exactly approve, he didn't object either, and I knew I had an accomplice in my mission. Together we waited, listening to the drips and trickles from the thawing snow, watching the moon appearing and disappearing among the gathering clouds. At last the lights went out, and soon afterwards I heard Maggie's soft tread passing my bedroom door. Then the worst of the waiting began. We had to give her time to get ready for bed; maybe read for a while, then get into a sound sleep.

I didn't want to be rumbled in what I was about to do. I think I must have dozed, because I got an awful jolt when Claus's shrill voice started up right next to my ear.

'I'm sure she's asleep now. She must be. Shall I go and see?'

I crept to the door and eased it open. The landing always had a light on in case Danny woke in the night and couldn't find his way around. Claus scuttled across the floor. The door to Maggie's room was closed but not latched, and Claus narrowed himself and squeezed through like ecto-plasm. A blink or two later and he came oozing back, then raced over to me. I picked him up.

'Out for the count,' he said. 'Snoring like a drunk.'

She was, too. I could hear it myself as soon as I troubled to listen.

'Right, then,' I said. 'To work.'

Back in my room, I wrapped up warm and then re-emerged like a thief in the shadows. Claus rode on my shoulder again, and we crept down to the front hall where the coats were hung. The light from the upstairs landing reached just far enough, and I could see Maggie's jacket— the top layer on an overloaded hook. I felt in the pocket and pulled out the contents. In my hand were two nails, a small stapler, a box of matches and a pipette. I returned them and tried the other pocket. A sticking-plaster, a glass marble, a tiny torch, a tissue and the smallest screwdriver I had ever seen. But no key.

'Blast!'

I put everything back and tried the top pocket. A ten pound note. Nothing else.

'She's not taking any chances,' I whispered to Claus. 'She must have hidden it somewhere.'

'Maybe she took it to bed with her?'

Before I could reply, Claus took a flying leap and landed on the bannister rail. He shot off like a tiny guided missile and soon disappeared around the bend in the stairs.

While he was gone I borrowed the little torch from Maggie's pocket and made a search of the kitchen. I opened every drawer and cupboard, every jar and bin and pot, and I looked into every jug and bowl and cup. Nothing.

But Claus was having better luck. If he hadn't squeaked I would have trodden on him as he came hurtling across the kitchen floor. The brass key was in his mouth.

'You're a star!' I hissed, picking him up and taking the key. He rubbed at his jaws with his pink paws.

'Ouch,' he said. 'Heavy.'

I sympathised. The equivalent for me would have been carrying a pick-axe in my teeth from here to the farmyard and back.

'Where was it?' I asked.

'Tied around her wrist with a rubber band.'

'You're not serious?'

He made a chopping motion with his long incisors. 'Neat and clean,' he said. 'She didn't feel a thing.'

It wasn't going to be so easy to put it back. But for the moment I couldn't let that bother me.

Claus ran up my clothes like a sailor in the rigging and took up his position beside my ear.

'What are we waiting for?' he said.

A wave of anxiety threatened to swamp me, but I resisted it and it subsided.

'Nothing,' I said. 'Nothing at all.'

two

The casual sloppiness of the garage seemed sinister to me, now that I knew how carefully it had been contrived. But Claus's cavalier attitude gave me courage, and I closed the door behind me and turned on the light. Immediately we entered a timeless zone. In a windowless building, day and night lose their meaning.

The key turned silently in the lock, as though all the parts were oiled. I pulled back the trap door; trunk, rags and all, and peered into the hole below.

A set of wooden steps ran down from the garage floor. There was a switch on the wall just below ground level, and I flicked it as we began to descend. Below me the lights came on, revealing a long corridor at the foot of the stairs with six doors leading off it, three on each side. It was more than a lab. It was a whole under-ground complex.

The first room I entered was lined with steel boxes. Wires ran from terminals on each one to a panel of dials and switches on the far wall. I read some of the labels beneath

them. POWER ON/OFF. SECONDARY SUPPLY. BACK-UP. EMER-
GENCY POWER.

I took another look at the boxes and saw now that they
were batteries; sturdy and sophisticated, built to last. Presumably the lab needed a steady supply of power and, since
the sources Fourth World relied upon were unpredictable,
a large storage capacity was needed.

I was pleased with my deduction and tried to explain it to
Claus, but he wasn't interested. He cut across me.

'Come on, come on. What's next?'

I closed the door carefully behind us and listened for a
while in the corridor before opening the next. That one
wasn't a lab, either. It was a study, or office, or library, or all
three combined. There were books everywhere, scattered
across both of the desks, stacked on the floor, and stuffed
every which way into the bookcases which covered two of
the walls. There were papers and journals; drifted up at the
backs of the desks, jammed into filing racks, heaped beside
the computers which hummed in their sleep.

Claus wanted to get out of here, too, but I was deter-
mined to have a look around. I ran my eyes over some of
the titles on the shelves: *Dictionary of DNA. Early Man And
His Forerunners. Techniques of Avian Genetics.* On a lower shelf
I spotted a book that I had once seen Mom reading, called
Chariots of The Gods. Beside it were others that looked like
popular reading; *Crop Circles: Fact Or Fabrication?* and *Lost
Civilisations.* There were a few science fiction books as well.

Even one that I had read myself: *2001*, by A.C. Clarke. I took it out and flipped through it. Inside the front cover someone had written his name. BERNARD RUSSELL. Other than that there was nothing remarkable about the book. It was just a cheap, well-thumbed paperback.

'Let's go, Christie. Let's go,' Claus nattered. I would have stayed longer; taken a look at some of the papers, but I couldn't think straight with his nagging.

We moved on. The third room was a bathroom. I was nervous enough to want to use it, but I was afraid the flush would make too much noise, and decided I could wait. The fourth room was full of caged animals. I got a glimpse of a terrier dog, a duck, a glass box that contained eggs of all different shapes and sizes, and something that might have been a fox. But the creatures made such a din when they saw us that I closed the door quickly, my nerves a-jangle.

We moved on. The next door, at last, opened on to the lab.

It wasn't exactly what I had expected. The only lab I had ever seen was the one at school, with its rows of benches and stools, its Bunsen burners and brown bottles and bell jars. This one was much more high-tech. There was a bank of electrical equipment against one wall; what looked like fridges and ovens. On a central platform were powerful microscopes and a whole array of glass and plastic syringes and containers of different shapes and sizes.

The office had been stale and lifeless, but this place was

277

full of activity, as though the work was continuing even as Maggie slept. Machines hummed and droned and buzzed. One blinked a blue light from time to time, and another, with an electronic display, seemed to be counting or timing something. But despite all this I was oddly disappointed. I had expected something much more dramatic, and more comprehensible, somehow. I had thought that if I only saw the lab, everything would become clear in a flash. But these machines and vessels and tools meant nothing to me.

I was ready to turn back, but Claus had spotted something that I hadn't. At the far end of the room, partly concealed by some white lab coats that were hanging on it, was another door.

I almost didn't go in; certain that it was just another washroom, or a storeroom or something. But Claus urged me on, and I opened the door and peeped in. It was neither of those things. It was a fully-equipped operating theatre.

There was a large steel table in the centre. Above it, a pair of overhead lights gazed down like gigantic insect eyes. At the head of the table stood a trolley and a drip stand, both of them sprouting tubes. Beside them stood a bulky machine with a TV screen, which I recognised from a medical programme I had watched. Ultrasound. On a workbench nearby were more plastic-wrapped syringes, an autoclave, and an array of surgical tools.

I couldn't make sense of it. What sort of operations could Maggie be performing in here? Was she operating on the animals' brains, somehow? I had heard about microchip implants. Maybe that was what she was doing, or something equally bizarre?

Claus tugged at my ear with tiny paws.

'What?' I said.

'Look,' he said.

'I *am* looking,' I said, scanning along the shelves of bottles and tubes and flasks, the boxes of needles and swabs and dressings.

'Not there!' shrieked Claus, and there was terror in his tiny voice. 'Behind you!'

I turned around and saw the reason for Claus's fear. On a deep shelf which ran the whole length of the wall above the door, stood a display of horrors. For a moment I couldn't take it in; it just looked like a row of huge bottles, filled with some kind of murky fluid. Then I saw what was in them. The results of Maggie's experiments.

They were all dead; little corpses preserved in yellowish fluid. I steeled myself to look more closely. Some of them seemed almost normal. There was a rat with a rather large head, and a chicken that appeared to be quite all right until I noticed that it had no eyes. But other things were desperately deformed. There was a cat that had something like hands instead of paws, a rabbit with an extra pair of legs sprouting from its shoulders, and a thing that looked like a fish with a dog's head.

There were worse things, too; things that I couldn't even begin to identify. But the worst of them all was the biggest of all the specimens. It was human, or nearly human, and about the size of a newborn infant. Its features were quite clear, and its milky eyes gazed into eternity. But there the clarity ended. The corpse's hands and feet were leathery and claw-like, and the whole of its body was covered with tiny quills, from which a fine, yellow down emerged, turned into hair-like strands by the fluid.

I was afraid I was going to throw up. Below my hairline, Claus was in a state of extreme agitation, running backwards and forwards along my collar, saying, 'Let's go, let's get out of here!'

I didn't need any more persuasion. A few seconds later we were back in the garage with the trap door closed and locked.

Claus ran down my arm, jumped on to the trunk, then vanished beneath the clutter in the corner. I called him three times, but he didn't reply. He had gone home, and he was staying there.

And I could think of no better plan.

four

But there was no way I could take Danny with me. I couldn't possibly show him what I had just seen, and he wouldn't understand if I tried to explain. I wasn't sure yet what I planned to do. It was all too much for me, and I felt too young and inexperienced to deal with it. I wanted to phone home, talk to Mom and Maurice about it all; see what they suggested. I knew they couldn't come for us, but maybe they'd send the police and they would sort out this mess.

Because now I knew what Maurice had been talking about when he said he could 'shop' Maggie. I knew nothing about the laws relating to scientific work, but I was certain that creating mutations had to be illegal.

I hoped the phone in Bettyhill would be working. I hoped Obi and Kanobi would remember me if I came across them in the dark, and that they would allow me to leave Fourth World. And I hoped that I wouldn't have to do it alone.

I woke Tina quietly. She sat bolt upright, staring into space.

'Christie. What is it?'

'You have to get up.'

She rubbed her eyes and yawned. 'I dreamt I was back in Dublin, on the street. I thought you were Ronan.'

'Shh!' I whispered, terrified that we would wake Maggie. 'There are terrible things going on here, Tina. I got into the lab. It's a chamber of horrors. She's experimenting on live animals!'

Tina stared at me, trying to absorb what I was saying.

'I don't believe Mother would do that,' she said, at last. 'What kind of experiments?'

She stared at me, wide-eyed, as I described what I had seen.

'I'll show you if you don't believe me,' I said.

But she shook her head. 'What makes you think Mother made them?'

'Of course she did! How else could they have got there?'

'She might have collected them,' said Tina. 'They used to have sideshows with stuff like that at fairs and circuses. She probably bought them from someone.'

'No,' I said. 'I'm sure she didn't. She has an operating theatre down there. Come and see.'

But Tina didn't want to know. She was determined to believe her own explanation, and nothing I said would convince her otherwise. I think she was asleep again before I even left the room.

It was all up to me then. I went back to my bedroom and went through what remained of the gear I had brought with me. There wasn't much: my penknife, pyjamas, the space-blanket. Inside a spare woolly sock I discovered the phonecard and, with a pang of guilt, the four letters for Bettyhill which I had never delivered. I was sorry to let the postmistress down, but I hadn't time to be bothered with them now.

I stuffed everything else into my pillowcase and pocketed the money that was left. I had intended to return it to Maggie, but now I was glad that I hadn't. If I wound up having to walk home, I was going to need it.

Someone else, would, too. Because I had already decided that I wasn't going to leave Fourth World alone.

As I slipped into the shed, Sparky woofed anxiously, but when I spoke to her she recognised my voice and went quiet. By the light of Maggie's torch I located Loki and, rubbing Sparky's head to distract her, I slipped the tiny pup into the pocket of my jacket. I knew she was too young to leave her mother, but I would get milk some-how along the way. And I needed her. Partly because she was my dog, and our attachment to each other was already strong. But there was another reason as well.

If anyone ever called my story into doubt, Loki would be my evidence.

I straightened up, whispered goodbye to Sparky, and stepped into the dark courtyard, on my way home.

five

But that was as far as I got.

'Hello, Christie,' said Maggie. 'Going somewhere?'

I didn't answer. Adrenalin was pumping through me, and my body was raring to make a run for it, but in the moonlight I could just make out the shadowy shapes of Obi and Kanobi, standing behind Maggie like henchmen.

'I think you have something belonging to me,' she said.

I felt in my pockets. I had three things if the money counted. Four, if Loki did.

I handed over the torch.

'That isn't what I had in mind,' she said.

I handed over the key, and she pocketed it.

'Where were you going?' she said. Her voice was calm and kind, and I was reminded of how I had felt about her since the first time I met her, and how she had let me down.

It hurt. Bitterness poisoned my voice. 'I'm going home.'

'But why creep about in the middle of the night? You're free to go home any time you like.'

'Oh yeah,' I snapped. 'You have no phone. There are no cars, no buses, no trains. I feel like a prisoner here. A slave.'

'Oh, Christie,' she said, and the sorrow in her voice sounded so genuine that it scratched my hurt feelings like sandpaper. 'You should have told me you were unhappy here. There are other ways to travel, you know?'

'Like what? Tony and trap?'

She turned to the west and the breeze lifted her thick hair and tossed it around her face.

'We're on an island, Christie,' she said. 'All around us are water and wind.'

'So what?' I asked, sounding like Tina. Like Tina *used* to sound.

'Have you ever travelled under sail?'

A boat. It hadn't crossed my mind.

'No.'

'If you want to go home I'll get you there. I promise you that. Even if I have to man the tiller myself. But you must let me show you something first.'

My hackles rose. 'What?'

'My lab.'

'Uh-uh,' I said. 'I've already seen it. You won't get me down there again in a fit.'

'I thought you wanted to know what we're doing here,' said Maggie. 'I'd like to explain it to you. Let you in on my secrets.' She paused, and when I said nothing she went on, 'I thought you were interested in science.'

I gave a humourless laugh which I hoped sounded scornful. 'Tell me your secrets and let me run off with them?'

'I have no reason to mistrust you, Christie. But perhaps you don't trust me?'

I found that I didn't. I had no intention of ending up on that steel table. But I was still overwhelmed by curiosity about the animals, and how they came to be able to talk. I thought about it for so long that the dogs got bored and flopped down at my feet with enormous sighs. Then I made up my mind.

'I'll come down to the lab with you. But only on one condition.'

'What's that?'

'Tina comes with us.'

I saw Maggie's white teeth flash in the moon-light as she smiled.

'Go and get her, then,' she said.

six

Even with Tina at my side I was petrified as I went back down the stairs below the garage. As we entered the lab my knees were weak, and I found myself listening out for the hiss of knockout gas, and watching Maggie like a hawk in case she grabbed a syringe and plunged it into my thigh. But all she did was clear a pair of tall stools so Tina and I could sit down. As for herself, she wandered around as she spoke to us; a woman in her element; as comfortable, I reflected, as an eel in mud.

'It's hard to know where to begin,' she said.

'At the beginning,' Tina suggested.

'But where is it?' said Maggie. 'Not easy to find.'

'Fourth World?'

But she said, 'No. Before that. I came from a line of chemists. That was where the money came from; the pharmaceutical industries that my grandparents owned. But I was always more interested in genetics than in chemistry, and that's what I studied at college. In Oxford. That's where I met Maurice.'

'Who's Maurice?' asked Tina.

'Danny's dad,' I said. 'What was he doing there?'

'Medicine,' said Maggie. 'He was one of their most promising students, despite the fact that he seemed to spend most of his life partying and acting the clown.'

I found it hard to imagine Maurice acting the clown, but I didn't say anything.

'We struck up a relationship and spent hours discussing the latest trends in medicine and genetic engineering and, when I suddenly came into a big inheritance, we decided to set up together. To combine our skills in a place where we wouldn't be watched too closely.'

'Fourth World,' said Tina.

Maggie nodded. 'We worked well together, Maurice and I,' she said, a little wistfully, I thought. 'We made mistakes, but we learnt from them. But after Danny was born, Maurice began to get cold feet. He found it difficult to accept Danny for what he was, and we began to have disagreements. Maurice wanted to call it a day and close the lab down, but I maintained that we had only just got established, and that we shouldn't be frightened off the work we were doing.'

Her gaze settled on the workbench beside me, but it was the past she was seeing.

'Misunderstandings arose, and one day, without warning, Maurice left, taking Danny with him.'

'Why didn't you go after him?' asked Tina, and there was an edge to her voice which made me remember her words about absent mothers, and the hurt that still surrounded the issue for her.

'I did,' said Maggie. 'But I couldn't find them. Maurice's parents put up a stone wall and refused to tell me where they were. There was nothing I could do. It wasn't until last year that he eventually contacted me.'

She turned to me.

'Your mother persuaded him,' she said. 'I'll always be grateful to her for that.'

Poor Mom. When they found out where we were, she would never be allowed to forget it.

'In the meantime,' Maggie went on, 'I was stuck. Alone up here with all the work and all the responsibility but no one to help. I was in despair; I nearly gave up. Then, one day, I was reading through a scientific journal and I came across a reference to Bernard.'

'Sandy's dad,' said Tina.

'That's right. The article concerned a debate over a paper he had written about his research. He claimed to have made one of the most significant discoveries in the history of mankind, but the scientific establishment had dismissed him as a crank, and he was unable to get funding or facilities to pursue his research. So I wrote to him.'

'But what was his discovery?' I said.

Maggie returned from the past and looked at me, her eyes bright with remembered excitement. 'He claimed,' she said, 'to have discovered the missing link.'

seven

Loki chose that moment to wake up and start crying. I had forgotten about her, and now I was worried that Maggie would be angry. But when I took the pup out of my pocket, she just smiled.

'Planning to take her with you?' she said.

'She's my dog,' I said, holding Loki up to my face. She wagged her tail and licked me, but she was clearly anxious as well.

'Ma, Ma, Ma,' she said.

We all laughed, and I hugged her tight.

'There you are,' said Maggie. 'She's the result of Bernard's research.'

'Really?' I said. Now it was getting interesting.

'I wrote to him and he sent me the paper that no one would publish. It described the work he had done on genetic analysis of early man and the apes that preceded him on the evolutionary ladder.'

Loki whimpered softly. I nestled her in the crook of my arm and stroked her little ears as Maggie continued.

'Bernard had isolated a specific gene that he believed was responsible for the big leap forward in evolution. He believed that this gene was responsible for reason and the capacity for language. Early man had this gene, but the apes didn't.'

'Wow,' said Tina.

'To be honest,' said Maggie, 'I was as sceptical about the work as the rest of the scientific community. But it didn't matter. Bernard's needs and mine fitted together perfectly. He needed facilities, I needed help with Fourth World and my own genetic work. I wrote to him with a proposal. It was risky, but it was worth it. He accepted.'

Maggie yawned and stretched. 'I need a coffee,' she said, and led the way into the last of the rooms that opened off the corridor; the one that Claus and I hadn't got round to exploring. It turned out to be a neat little kitchenette, with a tiny fridge, cooker and sink. Maggie put the kettle on, and while we waited for it to boil she became thoughtful and looked from Tina to me and back again.

'I'm giving you a lot of power over me,' she said. 'Letting you in on all this. My work here is . . . let's say . . . a little beyond medical convention. You could cause a lot of trouble for me if you wanted to.'

I had already worked that out, but I said nothing.

'I don't think you will, though,' she went on. 'I think that when you understand what I'm doing, you'll know why it has to be secret.'

She put coffee powder and sugar into three mugs and then, too impatient to wait for the kettle to boil, she poured warm water over them.

'Bernard helped me with my work to begin with,' she said. 'That was the deal. We . . . well . . . we engineered Sandy and Colin, among other things.'

'Engineered?' I said.

Maggie hesitated. 'I really do hope I can trust you,' she said. 'You wanted to know how Sandy learnt to kick so powerfully, and how she got to the top of that tree so fast, didn't you?'

I nodded, eagerly.

Maggie gulped down her cup of tepid coffee before she answered. 'Sandy jumped to the top of that tree. Everything about her is human, except for one thing. She has the muscle tissue of a frog.'

eight

I was dumbstruck, but Tina just laughed. 'That's why the animals call her Sprog,' she said. 'That's why she looks so skinny and . . .' She stopped, aware that she might offend. But Maggie finished for her.

'Weird, yes. But she was a spectacular success, all the same. Wouldn't you agree?'

'I suppose so,' I said. 'Although I wouldn't much fancy having to stay hidden all my life.'

Maggie's expression darkened, and I hurriedly went on. 'But how did you do it?'

'I can show you the technical details some other time,' said Maggie. 'For the moment all you need to know is that if you incorporate genetic material into the nucleus of a cell, it will join with the DNA that's already there. That's how genetic modification happens.'

'You can do that here? In the lab?'

'That's right. We isolate specific genes. Introduce them into host cells.'

'But what about the animals?' said Tina. 'I want to know how come my babies can talk.'

'That was Bernard's bit,' said Maggie. 'After what we had already done it was relatively simple to apply my technique to his requirements.' She gave a wry smile. 'Do you know, I only did it to keep my side of the bargain? I never believed for a minute that it would work.'

'But it did,' said Tina.

'We had our share of mistakes, but that's only to be expected. And as you can see, we eventually succeeded in isolating exactly the strand of DNA that we wanted. Now we have an eighty to ninety per cent success rate.'

'But why does it all have to be so secret?' I said. 'I mean, if I was Bernard, I couldn't wait to prove that I was right. Show all those stuffy old professors where to get off.'

Maggie nodded. 'We discussed it for hours. Days and nights, sometimes. But in the end we both agreed that we wouldn't go public. For one thing, it would have been the end of our secrecy, and we weren't at all sure that we had come to the end of our work together.'

'And the other reason?' asked Tina.

'The animals themselves,' said Maggie.

Tina must already have thought of that. Sometimes I wondered how I could be so slow. 'People would exploit them, wouldn't they?' she said. 'Make them perform, or do all kinds of dirty work that no one else wants to do.'

'That was our thinking, yes,' said Maggie. 'Even worse things, perhaps. I shudder to think about what the military might use them for if they knew.'

'Spies,' said Tina. 'Messengers.'

But I had been raised on computer games. 'Kamikaze grenades,' I said. 'Walking mines.'

Maggie nodded. 'You see?' she said.

I stroked Loki's back. I had no problem with that. How could I? The talking animals were a joy, and anything that protected them from exploitation was all right by me. But the things in the jars still haunted me.

'What about *your* side of the work?' I asked. 'Are you still making . . .' I wanted to say 'freaks', or 'mutants', but neither word seemed fair to Danny or Sandy.

Maggie shook her head.

'After Colin was born I thought we could create anything we wanted to. I was ambitious, and I was wrong.' She paused, and an uncharacteristic sadness dragged at her features. 'You probably saw, Christie,' she said. 'My little bird.'

I knew what she was talking about. The feathered baby. At the same moment I understood what she had intended. She had been trying to create a winged child. An angel on the face of the earth.

But she had failed, and the grisly spectre returned to my mind.

'Why do you keep them?' I cried out, surprised at the

strength of my emotion. 'All those terrible mistakes, lined up in there like . . . like gruesome trophies!'

Maggie shook her head, her face still slack with sorrow.

'It's not like that, Christie. It's just the opposite. I keep them there to watch over my work. My little twisted gods. In case I should ever be tempted to make the same mistakes again.'

part
eleven

Maggie proved as good as her word. The very next morning, as soon as the chores were out of the way, she brought me into the lab again and gave me a tour of the equipment. I saw the genetic material for myself in the electron microscope, and she showed me how, using an array of enzymes, small segments of it could be separated off, to be added later to the primary cell of the host embryo.

'But I don't understand why the cell accepts it,' I said. 'Normally cells fight off foreign bodies.'

'No one knows, really,' said Maggie. 'Apparently the DNA isn't recognised as foreign. All we know is that it works.'

'It's creepy,' I said. 'It's like playing God.'

Maggie looked at me closely for a moment, then led the way into the operating theatre. I was careful not to look at the sinister reminders of her failures.

'This is where we remove the eggs from the mother animal,' she said. 'They're fertilised and modified in the lab, then replaced in the mother's womb.'

I had a hundred questions about that part of the process, but I realised just in time that Maggie had herself been one of those mothers, not just once, but on several occasions. I was fairly sure that she would have no problem in talking about it, but those details would be a bit too intimate for my liking.

I must have blushed again, because she gave a roar of laughter.

'Good old Christie,' she said, and scruffed up my hair.

I shrugged her off, even though I was secretly pleased.

'Why didn't you want to show me before?' I asked. 'Why all the secrecy?'

'You forced my arm,' she said. 'If you hadn't, I would never have shown you. This place is my life. It could all be blown apart so easily.'

She led the way out of the theatre and closed the door behind us. Then she looked at me, searchingly. 'Can I trust you, Christie?' she said. 'I know that Tina will never say a word, but I'm not so sure about you.'

I wasn't so sure about me, either. I could have said anything; made her any kind of an empty promise, but I knew it wasn't what she wanted. She was looking for something more fundamental in me; some core of integrity that she could rely upon. But I couldn't find it within me, and I couldn't lie, either.

As though she was reading my thoughts, Maggie went on, 'I meant what I said yesterday. You're free to come and go as you like. No one will stop you. You have no reason to fear me.'

I believed her. I thought she was going to ask me again for some kind of assurance, but she didn't. She just led the way out of the lab, up the stairs, and into the welcome light of the soft, spring day.

two

And now I couldn't put it off any longer. As soon as lunch was over, I went up to my room and collected the letters for Bettyhill, the phonecard and the money. But I didn't take the rest of my things and I didn't take Loki. This time, at least, I intended to come back.

Oggy came with me to show me the way. As we crossed the boundary of Fourth World, Darling dropped out of the trees and joined us. She hadn't been around much, lately, and I was happy to see her. As we walked along the side of the glen it was almost like the old days, with Oggy scouting ahead and Darling mocking the skylarks as they sang in the heights, just inches beneath the low, white clouds.

There were still patches of snow, but it was melting fast, and little streams ran everywhere down the hillsides. Some of them were deep, and before long I gave up trying to keep my feet dry. Oggy splashed and slobbered, and Darling dive-bombed him, and I thought about what would happen if people knew about them. For their sakes, and for Loki and Tony and Iggy's new brood, I could never blow the whistle on Fourth World, whatever I thought about the other stuff. It made me feel anxious, though, about phoning home. I knew that Maurice didn't feel the same way.

As we neared the first of the village houses, Darling banked away and went off about some other business. Oggy stayed with me, following at my heels like an obedient pet.

There was no one in the first house, or the second, and they both looked forlorn, as though they had been deserted through no fault of their own. At the next house I could hear the sound of a television, and my knock was soon answered by a middle-aged woman in rolled-up sleeves and an apron. She looked extremely suspicious until I showed her the letters, and then she ushered me ahead of her into the sitting-room, where an open fire and the television competed for attention.

'Let me get my glasses, now,' she said. I watched the screen as she searched for them. There were pictures of the Prime Minister heading off to Brussels in an army jet to discuss the energy crisis with other European leaders. There were pictures that reminded me of the streets of Inverness; more civil unrest; more soldiers. After that there were scenes of policemen managing queues outside supermarkets, of empty shelves, of army food convoys travelling along deserted motorways.

The woman had found her glasses. She examined the battered letters carefully. 'This one's for my cousin,' she said. 'And this one's for my sister-in-law. Nothing for me.'

The television was showing tractors busy throughout the land, ploughing up set-aside to grow more food for the population.

'These people are gone,' the woman went on. 'And Donie lives three miles along the coast. You won't want to be walking out there, I'm sure.'

She began squirrelling around among the clutter on the mantelpiece. 'I'm sure to see Donie in the village. And I may as well take care of the others, as well. Save you the trouble.'

She had two pound coins in her hand. She was about to give them to me and I was about to refuse. But she hesitated. 'Where is it you're staying, now?'

'Along the Glen,' I said. 'With Maggie Taylor.'

The pound coins went into the woman's apron pocket, and the friendly smile slid off her face.

'Well,' she said, 'You'd better be getting back there, then.'

I followed Oggy along the road, wishing that people could understand that, whatever Maggie might be doing, it posed no threat to them. It made Fourth World into a kind of island, surrounded by hostility. I wondered how Maggie stuck it; how Sandy survived without friends; whether there might be real danger of raids by local people if the food situation didn't improve. And then I saw something which drove all other thoughts out of my mind.

Oggy had led me to the phone box.

three

I discovered what cold feet meant, and nearly turned back. It was only the thought that the phones might be down that gave me the courage to step forward.

But they weren't. The connection went through first time. The answer-phone was on again, and Mom's voice explained that they had gone to stay with her sister on the family farm. She repeated the number. I breathed on the window and wrote it on the glass with my finger.

I dialled again, and doodled nervously on the glass as it rang. I expected my aunt or my uncle to answer, but they didn't. Mom did. When she heard my voice, she said, 'Christie!' It was like a sigh, a cry, and a laugh all rolled into one. 'Where are you?'

My heart led me. 'We're safe, Mom. Safe and warm and well-fed.'

'But where?'

'It doesn't matter. How are you? And Maurice?'

'We're fine.'

I could hear Maurice in the background, saying, 'Is it them? Is it them?'

'Things aren't so bad in the country,' Mom went on. 'There's more trouble in the towns.'

I could hear Maurice again, and Mom said, 'Please tell us where you are.'

'We're with . . . with friends.'

'What friends?'

'You don't know them,' I began, but Maurice's voice, at the receiver now, interrupted me.

'You're in Scotland, aren't you?'

I hesitated, and by the time I tried to deny it, it was too late.

'We found a map in Danny's room,' said Maurice. 'You had it all planned, didn't you? You and her?'

'No! It didn't happen like that at all!'

Maurice ploughed on, as though he wasn't listening to me at all.

'We can't come for you, you know. Not yet, anyway. But I'm going to send the police.'

Anxiety began to rise into my chest again, but then a strange thing happened. My fear fell away and I knew I was not the sullen, lazy boy that had left home those long weeks ago. I was someone else, now; someone who had made an incredible journey, come close to death, and learnt how to fend for himself.

My thoughts cleared and I remembered the television

pictures I had just seen. 'The police aren't going to be interested,' I said. 'Not with all this other stuff going on. Besides, you should see Danny. He's never been happier, Maurice. He's found a purpose in life.'

Maurice went ominously quiet. I noticed that my card was running out.

'What purpose?' he said, breathlessly.

'He's working in the garden.'

Maurice let his breath out, and as he spoke again, his tone had quite changed. Suddenly we were speaking man to man.

'Listen to me, Christie,' he said. 'You may be right about the police. But will you promise me one thing?'

'What?'

'Look after Danny. Don't take your eyes off him. Maggie's persuasive, I know that. But she's not to be trusted. You understand? There are things you don't know.'

The read-out flashed down from £1.20 to £1.00.

'Like what?' I said.

'A lot of things.'

'My money's running out, Maurice.'

It galvanised him, and he blurted it all out. 'When he was a baby, only two months old, she tried . . .'

'It's nearly gone.'

'She tried to drown him!'

I was shocked into silence.

'Watch him, Christie. Promise me.'

'I promise.'

And then Mom was on again.

'When will you be coming home?'

'Whenever I can, Mom.'

'Be careful, Christie. Be careful.'

And Maurice said, 'Look after yourself as well!'

Then the line went dead, and the long miles were back between us again.

four

My heart was in my boots as I trudged back along the glen, and my mind was somewhere down there, too, trying to find it. And failing. It wasn't only Fourth World that was incomprehensible to me. All worlds were. Not least my own. How could I possibly find truth in the midst of so much chaos? Every time I thought I had found it, something else came along and proved me wrong. I didn't want to believe what Maurice had said, but I couldn't dismiss it, either. Maybe I was a fool to trust anyone or anything. Even Oggy, trotting dogwise ahead of me, was an impenetrable mystery again. I turned everything over in my mind, but it made me more uneasy, not less. Because something in that missing link business didn't quite ring true. There was a failure of logic somewhere in the story, but at that moment in the damp, quiet glen, I couldn't locate it. The only missing links I could find were the ones in my brain. I couldn't think straight at all.

As I helped Danny wash his muddy hands that evening, I made a silent promise to him. Whether Maurice's words were true or not, I would never leave Fourth World without him, and I would watch him night and day.

At dinner, Tina made an announcement that turned the meal into a celebration. One of Iggy's babies had said its first word.

Maggie was ecstatic.

'You realise what it means?' she said. 'The gene can be transmitted through the bloodlines. It could mean that every one of the talking animals can have talking offspring.'

'A new world order!' said Sandy.

'Hope they'll use their intelligence better than humans have,' said Tina.

And Danny, because everyone else seemed so happy, just laughed and laughed and laughed.

Everyone except me, that was. I accepted the drop of champagne that Maggie gave us all, and I drank the piglets' health. But I was still wrestling with the problem of the missing link. There was definitely something about the story that was wrong.

It wasn't until the washing-up was over and I was about to take Danny off to bed that the penny finally dropped.

'That's what I don't understand,' I said, turning back into the room as I spoke. 'You've found the missing link, so you say, and you've isolated it and put it into the animals?'

'That's right,' said Maggie.

'Then where have Bernard and Colin gone? What is there left to find?'

Maggie smiled. 'So there is something between your ears, after all,' she said. I fought down another blush, unsuccessfully.

'Sit down, Christie,' she went on. 'You, too, Tina. You may need to be sitting down to hear this.'

We all took our places again and Maggie drained the last of the champagne into her glass. Then she turned to me.

'You said something this morning that I thought was quite shrewd. You said that what we are doing in the lab is a bit like playing God.'

I nodded, feeling more flattered than I deserved to.

'In a sense you're right,' Maggie went on. 'And some say that we're interfering in a process that has always been taken care of by nature; or by God, if you prefer.'

Tina wasn't looking at Maggie, but I could tell she was all ears. Sandy stifled a yawn. She had heard all this before.

'What we've done here may be unethical,' Maggie continued. 'Maybe you think so, Christie?'

At that moment, at least, I did. But I just shrugged.

'One of the reasons I've been able to live with my conscience is that neither I, nor Maurice, has ever looked for any profit from anything we've done.'

'You hardly need to,' said Tina, with a hint of her old bitterness.

'There are other kinds of profit,' said Maggie. 'Prizes.

Fame. Power. But anyway, that's neither here nor there. There's another reason as well, based upon a conclusion that Bernard and I reached in our work together.'

'What's that?' I asked.

'If it's true that we're playing God,' said Maggie, 'then we have reason to believe that we're not the first ones to have done it.'

'What?' said Tina and I together.

'If our research has been conducted properly, it seems that someone else once played God with us.'

I lay on the floor in Danny's room, where I had made up my bed for the night. The moon was grinning at me through his window, taunting me to come out into its realm again. But there would be no more midnight jaunts, not for the moment, anyway. I was staying where Danny was; night and day.

I hadn't understood much of what Maggie had gone on to tell us that evening. A lot of it was technical stuff about the structure of DNA and how it created the blueprint for the different forms of life on the planet. But I think I had understood the overall results. She and Bernard had studied their missing link gene and found it was in some way subtly different from other genes. There was nothing quite like it in any living creature, and they had gone into meticulous studies of ape genetics to try and find if there was anything around that might be a precursor to it. But there was nothing remotely like it. The gene seemed not to have evolved, but to have appeared from nowhere. The only conclusion they could come to was that someone, or something, must have put it there. So Bernard, with Colin and a handful of animals, had set off for the places where prehistoric man was believed to have originated, looking for evidence that some other form of life, more advanced than ours, had been there.

It made my mind jump through hoops; it was surely too far-fetched to be true. I wondered how much more I was going to have to absorb on my way towards coming to terms with Fourth World.

There was something comforting about being there in Danny's room, listening to his deep, slow breathing as he slept. He hadn't understood a word that Maggie had said, and I was glad that his innocence protected him from it, because it meant he had no insight into what he really was. Not a gardener, as he thought, but an experiment gone wrong. And one, if what Maurice said was true, that his mother had tried to get rid of.

six

I woke in the morning to the sound of Danny singing as he got himself dressed. I wished I could feel as bright in the mornings, but I didn't, and I pulled my covers up over my head and tried to go back to sleep.

Maggie came in soon afterwards.

'Who's that?' she said, giving me a prod with her toe.

I revealed my face.

'What are you doing in here?'

'Couldn't sleep,' I said. 'Had a nightmare.'

'And you thought your big brother would protect you?'

Danny laughed and assured me he would die for me.

'Sorry, Christie,' said Maggie. 'I'm not being very sympathetic. Was it a bad one?'

'Pretty bad.' And then, before I could stop myself, I said, 'I dreamt you tried to drown Danny.'

Danny laughed again, but Maggie didn't. It was the first time I had ever seen her lose possession of herself. An expression of shock swept over her face, and then her features stiffened as she tried to mask it. Without a word, she left the room. Danny lumbered after her, leaving one sock and both his boots behind him.

My heart was pounding. I had hit on some truth, I knew. For a moment or two I lay there, staring blindly at the ceiling. Then, remembering myself, I jumped up, threw on my clothes, and followed the others down to the kitchen.

It was as though nothing had happened. Maggie was her usual, shining self, standing over the porridge on the range. Danny was whistling his football anthem, fairly tunelessly, over and over again. After a few minutes I realised he was whistling continuously, without taking a breath, and that Maggie had the fancy timer out again. When he ran out of steam and began giggling, the display read three minutes and fifty-two seconds. Not as long as he could hold his breath for, but no mean feat all the same.

Tina came in with one of the pups and sat in her place at the table.

'No animals in the kitchen,' said Maggie.

'Oggy and Itchy are allowed in,' said Tina.

'They're different,' said Maggie.

'Muffin's different as well,' said Tina, staying where she was, cradling the wagging pup. The little show of rebellion gave me heart. I winked at her and she winked back. Maybe there was hope for Tina yet.

When Sandy came in with the milk we sat down to eat,

and as soon as we had finished, Maggie began to organise the day.

'I think we can begin digging in the manure for the potatoes,' she said. 'What do you think, Danny?'

'Manure?' said Danny. 'Digging it into the ground?'

'That's right. I'll show you how. Maybe Sandy and Christie will fetch it for us?' She looked at me. 'From the muck-heap beside the sheds?'

'Maybe I'll help Danny with the digging,' I said. 'Maybe Tina can help Sandy?'

Maggie went quiet and turned a penetrating gaze upon me that I could not meet. Then she said, 'Change of plan. I think it's time we all went on a little outing.'

'Where?' said Tina.

'Magical mystery tour,' said Maggie. 'Let's go.'

We left the breakfast things where they were and Maggie led the way out of the back door. Danny followed.

'Hang on a minute,' I said. 'Danny's got no shoes.'

'Never mind,' said Maggie. 'He won't be needing them where we're going.'

I ran back to get jackets. By the time I came out again the up-and-over door of the garage was open and Maggie was starting the engine of the car. I stood by the open passenger door.

'But it's not allowed,' I called in to her. 'You told us that yourself!'

'Get in,' said Maggie.

There was no arguing. Danny was pushing me aside to get in the front, and everybody else was already piling in. Oggy and Itchy were sharing my seat in the back, deliriously excited.

As I shoved them aside to get in, Darling appeared from nowhere, flashed through the last few inches of the closing door and whirred around the confined space for a moment before settling on Danny's headrest. Beside me, Tina was hugging the anxious pup and making soothing noises. But as soon as the car left the garage she began to sing, very quietly, 'Goody, goody, two shoes.'

I gave her a dig with my elbow, but I didn't have the heart for sparring.

There were too many other things on my mind.

seven

Whatever worries I had about the police were soon submerged by the greater anxiety about where Maggie was taking us. We sped along the empty lanes, confident of meeting no other traffic, and before long we had left the glen behind us and were sailing along the coast road.

'Where are we going?' I asked. But Maggie didn't reply, and no one else seemed in the slightest bit concerned.

We passed a couple of cyclists, one with a heavy basket, the other with a jumble of fishing tackle. Outside a little croft, a woman put down her spade to give us all a cheery wave. Otherwise the whole area seemed deserted. I found myself wishing we would meet a police car. There was something scary about Maggie's mood. She drove almost recklessly, propelled by some fierce passion that I couldn't understand. I would have preferred to be arrested.

As soon as the sea came into view, Danny stopped whistling and singing and slipped into the mesmerised state that I recognised from our journey. I put a reassuring hand on his shoulder, but the sea commanded his entire attention. I don't think he even knew I was there.

For a mile or so the road went inland again. I was relieved to be leaving the coast, though I couldn't have told anyone why. But then Maggie swung sharply left, on to a narrow, crumbling road which ended up, a few minutes later, beside a tiny, stone pier.

She drove right on to it and turned off the engine. A couple of ruined cottages overlooked the sea, and an ancient fishing boat sat on its bare ribs on the stony shore. The place had a desolate, abandoned air that gave me the creeps, and from their motionless silence I suspected that the others felt the same way. Even Maggie seemed daunted, but she drove herself into action and opened her door.

'Out,' she ordered. 'Everyone out!'

We spilt out of the back, but Danny was frozen to the spot. Maggie came round to his side and, with a trusting expression that sent a pang of apprehension through my diaphragm, he allowed her to lead him out.

'Why don't you let him stay in the car?' I said. 'He's got no shoes.'

Maggie didn't answer. I said it again.

'He's got no shoes! Where are you going with him?' I ran around in front of them, trying to bar their way. 'Why have you brought us here?'

'Trust me,' said Maggie. 'This isn't for you, or for me. This is for Danny.'

I didn't trust her. Not for a moment. But I didn't know what to do. Sandy was right beside me. If I tried to stop them with force, she would have knocked me flat in a split second. It was like the beginning of the journey all over again. I didn't want this to happen, but there was nothing I could do to stop it. I was helpless.

Maggie and Danny stopped at the edge of the pier. Danny stood like a statue, except that I could see the tension; the tiny tremor of emotion that affected every fibre of his being. To my relief, Maggie stepped away from him and stood at a short distance, watching him intently.

A mild swell was breaking against the pier. Danny watched it.

'What's going on?' said Tina. There was a hint of irritation in her voice. It was cold, and she was trying to keep the whimpering pup out of the brisk breeze which snatched this way and that. I remembered that Danny's jacket was in the car, and was about to go and get it when, without warning, he jumped.

I sprang to the edge of the pier. His head was still above the water, and he had a wild, faraway look in his eyes.

And then he went under.

For a long moment we all stood still, rooted to the stones where we stood. Then Tina stepped forward and we both yelled at the same time.

'Danny!'

Oggy plunged in and, a second later, Itchy followed. They

swam out to where he had been and circled in the water, but it was clear that they could see nothing of him. I turned to Maggie.

'Help him!' I shouted. 'Get him out of there!' But there was a small, secret smile on her face, and she shook her head.

How could I have let it happen? Even when I had been warned; when I knew she had tried it before. I ran up and down the edge of the stones, peering into the dark water, willing him to come up again and get a grip on the wall. The dogs were swimming further from the pier now, ducking their heads under the surface to look beneath the water. Above them, Darling darted and hovered, darted and hovered, covering large areas of the harbour in her aeriel search. But none of them were finding any sign of Danny. He must have gone down like a lump of concrete.

Suddenly Tina was beside me. She thrust the frightened puppy into my hands, shrugged off her jacket and began to wrestle with the laces of her beloved Doc's. Wherever her courage had gone to on the night the intruders came to Fourth World, it had returned in no small measure.

The things she had said about us along the way were forgotten; negated by her actions. She wasn't going to let Danny drown. She was going in after him.

But she never touched the water. In a single, impossible jump, Sandy was at her side.

'Don't get yourself wet,' she said. 'There's no point.'

Tina shoved her away, but Sandy bounced back again and grabbed her by the wrists. Tina thrashed and wriggled, but she was no match for Sandy's frog strength. I was about to go and help, when Maggie put a restraining hand on my arm.

'Don't worry,' she said. 'Danny isn't drowning.'

'Not drowning?' I snapped, my terror raising the pitch of my voice by at least an octave. 'Where is he, then? Where is he?'

I turned to face her and she gripped me with her gaze; strong and steady. And totally, utterly trustworthy. Like a holy shiver which began in my spine, the truth began to dawn. About Danny, and why he looked so weird, and why he could hold his breath for so long.

eight

And as though my thoughts needed another shove, he emerged at that moment. He didn't just surface; he launched himself up and above the waves, doubled in the air, and plunged back in again, back down to the depths.

Tina saw it as well, and her sharp mind grasped for meaning.

'Fish genes,' she said. 'You gave him fish genes.'

She was nearly right, but not quite.

He appeared again beside us, holding on to the uneven wall, splattering us with cold drops as he shook the water from his hair. He was laughing and crying, wild with excitement and joy. It wasn't his fear of the water that had upset him so much when he saw the sea. It was his desire for it. And Maggie hadn't tried to drown him, either. She had tried to prove that the experiment had worked.

Tina helped Oggy and Itchy up on to the pier. Danny headed for deeper water, leaping and diving, gliding through the waves with a grace he would never have on land. I remembered what he had said, standing on the shore outside Inverness.

'The big sea, Christie. People can't live in it.'

I thought it had been his way of communicating his fear, but I was wrong. He had been repeating what Maurice must have told him, again and again, whenever he had expressed his instinctive yearning for the ocean. If it hadn't been for Mom persuading Maurice to contact Maggie, and if it hadn't been for Darling and Oggy coming to collect us, Danny would have lived his whole life without ever knowing what he was.

Because Maurice hadn't trusted in what he had helped to create. He had chickened out; kept him hidden for all those years; denied him the chance to use his phenomenal lungs for their innate purpose.

But Maggie had believed in him. She had promised to show him what he was, and now she had. Not disabled. Not a gardener. Not a mistake, either. It was on the tip of my tongue when Maggie spoke.

'My dolphin boy,' she said. 'Thank you for bringing him home.'

A dolphin boy. The Yeti. Merpeople.
What other secrets will the friends of Fourth World
uncover in their search for the missing link?

Read on for a sneak peek
at the next gripping adventure in

Only Human
Book Two in the Missing Link Trilogy

one

We ate no meat of any kind in Fourth World, but our dairy and our gardens provided for most of our needs. The rest, the best, came from the Atlantic.

Danny was our fisherman. He went out at night when there was no danger that anyone would see what happened when he entered the water. On land he was awkward; a lumbering hulk of a teenager who somehow wasn't put together quite right, all out of step with himself and everyone else. But at sea, the dolphin genes that had been given to him before his birth came into their own. In the cold waters of the Atlantic, Danny was in his element.

Sometimes he stayed there for hours, swimming far out into the deepest, darkest currents where the herring ran, and the cod and wild salmon. He could have lived at sea, he told us. But he always came back, lugging his catch along the silent glen in the dark, creeping through the sleeping house to his bed before the birds began to sing.

Once I walked down the path with him, just for company's sake. It was a clear, still night and the sea was quiet, examining the stars that lay reflected on its dark surface like new ideas. We sat on the shore together, examining them too, until Danny said, 'There's something out there that sings.'

'Sings?' I said. 'Is it the whales, Danny?'

He shook his head. 'Whales sing, and dolphins do, too. But this is different. This is something . . .'

He looked into my face and then past it, and I waited for the word he was searching for. But he didn't find it.

'Something else,' was all he said.

two

It was early summer, and I was in the garden sweating over my hoe when Loki came hurtling down the hillside towards me.

'Thither-up!' she panted. 'Crampy gurgletube!'

I put aside the hoe and reached out a hand to her, but she was twisting around my legs like a small, dark tornado.

'Loki, stop,' I said, managing to grab hold of an ear. 'What's happening?'

She yelped and crouched at my feet.

'Whisker-hunt,' she said.

'Whose whiskers?' I asked. 'What have you done?'

She tried to mime it, racing up and down, leaping and pouncing, then gazing intently at the fallen hoe and wagging her tail. But the little drama was meaningless to me. I sighed and shook my head.

'I don't understand, Loki.'

She looked sad and perplexed, and my heart ached for her. There had been an unusual connection between us since we had first met, a few days after she was born. We had both known it. She was my dog, I was her boy. We had rapidly become inseparable. She was the brightest of the litter from the very start, streets ahead of her brothers and sisters in learning how to talk and to count and to work things out for herself. Until the accident, that was.

It still sent a shock through my veins when I remembered it. Sandy and I had been out in the woods all day, working one at each end of the bush saw. We had put up a mighty heap of firewood and I was exhausted. Sandy's frog muscle seemed to give her enormous stamina as well as strength, and working with her was like trying to keep pace with a machine. So I was relieved when Tony arrived with his little cart to bring home the logs.

He stood patiently in the shafts while we loaded up. Sandy picked and tossed with her usual vigour, but my arms were like jelly after the day's work, and I was completely butter-fingered. Loki realised I was in trouble and started retrieving the logs I dropped, even though she could barely get her little jaws around them. She was about three months old at the time.

I dropped one too many. The last one rolled under Tony's feet, and he decided to help, too, by pawing it back out to me. But Loki went for it at the same time, and Tony's hoof connected with her skull instead of the log.

He was mortified, poor thing. He thought he had killed her. So did I. She hadn't even yelped. She just sprawled where she had fetched up, quivering slightly. Her tongue was lolling and her eyes were open, but there was no sign of intelligence in them. I knelt beside her, frantic with concern. She was breathing, and her heart was beating. There was some chance, at least.

I forgot my exhaustion and ran home with her to Maggie. She laid Loki out on the kitchen table and examined her minutely. There was a soft swelling on the side of her head, and Maggie said that the bone had caved in underneath it. She made the pup comfortable in a box above the range, but confessed that she didn't hold out much hope for her.

I stayed up after the others had gone to bed, and draped Loki across my knees on the kitchen floor. I knew that she could hear me, even if she couldn't answer, and I talked to her non-stop about all the things we had done together and all the things we would still do, if only she would come back from whatever between-worlds place it was that she had gone to.

And she did come back. The next morning she was trying to lift her head, and her feet were twitching as though she were dreaming, or trying to run back to us from her waiting death. Over the next few days she managed to sit up, and I fed her with milk and soft flakes of fish. But she could neither speak nor understand what was said to her.

I couldn't be a full-time nurse to her. I was needed outside in the gardens. It was Tina who had the idea of leaving the radio on to keep her company, and Maggie who extended the idea and suggested tapes instead, to re-establish Loki's vocabulary. Maggie loved to listen while she was working, and had a small library of books on tape down in the lab. So, for the next few weeks, Loki lived in the sitting room, and while the rest of us were out at work, she kept company with Shakespeare and Tolstoy, Barrett Browning and the Brontes, Melville and Manley Hopkins.

It worked.

Well, almost.

'Try again, Loki,' I said, laying a hand on her head.

'Wurra-wurra-wurra,' she barked, chasing some imaginary creature around in small circles.

'Relax, Loki. Calm down.'

She parked herself tight against my legs and gazed up into my eyes.

'Hackle-scrap,' she said. 'Timorous tremblepuss.'

'Puss?' I asked.

She resorted to mimicry. The plaintive little sound was far easier to understand than all her previous efforts.

'Miaow?'

Loki led the way back up the hill-side and I followed her. I didn't like to admit it but she was becoming a bit of a liability. The blow to her head had affected more than her ability to form sentences. It seemed to have knocked a lot of the sense out of her as well.

All the animals of Fourth World learned to follow certain basic codes of behaviour. You didn't steal things. You didn't go charging all over the vegetable gardens, but kept to the paths. You didn't get into fights with other animals; not serious ones, anyway. Even Sparky, and Obi and Kanobi, who were Loki's relations and weren't talking dogs, understood these things. But Loki didn't.

Nor did she understand about meal-times or bed-times, or about the difference between night and day. All the animals had their own bowls and their own beds, but Loki was notorious for taking the wrong ones and created constant friction among the animals. The humans, too. She would steal food from the table at every opportunity, and tear around the house in the middle of the night, shouting 'Roustabout!' or 'Moonstalking!' or 'Man-the-barricades!'

We had tried putting her outside at night, but that was worse. Every sound she heard became a threat to Fourth World, and she ran around and barked incessantly, annoying everyone and making it impossible for Obi and Kanobi and Oggy and Itchy to get on with the real work of listening out for threatening sounds.

And although nobody ever blamed me, I felt responsible all the same. Loki was my dog. More and more, as time went on, she was becoming my problem.

'Hi, Christie!'

I turned and saw Sandy bounding towards me across the steep fields. In three or four more powerful jumps she was at my side.

'Where are you going?'

I nodded towards Loki, ahead of me on the hill-side. 'She seems to have found more trouble.'

'What's new?' said Sandy and set off again, up the hill ahead of me.

I followed, annoyed by my own pathetic, human pace. I had grown fond of Sandy over the months that I had been at Fourth World, but it didn't mean she didn't get on my nerves. I was well aware of how much stronger and faster she was than me, but I couldn't see why she had to keep on rubbing it in. At least, at times like this one I couldn't. In the quiet of my own thoughts I understood it very well.

At the top of the hill she stopped and called back to me. 'Come on, slow-coach!'

'All right, all right,' I called back. 'I'm only human, you know!'

She was well ahead of me again by the time I reached the heather-clad slopes above the meadows. Loki was with her, and came haring back to lick my hand and hurry me along.

'King's high-by-way,' she said. 'Squeezle-tib liberation crusade.'

'OK, Loki. I'm coming. I'm coming.'

'Suffocat!' she said. 'Urgent-emergency!'

Then she was gone again, jinking along the twisting path like a hunted hare, heading for the dam. I followed as quickly as I could, astonished, as usual, by her boundless energy.

I didn't know where she got it from and sometimes, I had to admit, it was worrying. I couldn't count the number of times I had lectured her on the importance of staying close to the house and of never, never talking in front of anyone who wasn't one of us; part of the Fourth World family. She understood, as she understood most things that were said to her, but there was no way of knowing whether she remembered. I kept my concerns to myself, but I was sure the disastrous possibilities must have occurred to the others as well.

It was crucial to our existence here at Fourth World that no one should discover what Maggie and her partner, Bernard, had produced. If the outside world found out about the missing link, the gene that enabled animals to speak and reason as humans did, there was no telling what might happen. Only one thing was certain. Our peaceful, self-sufficient life here would come to an abrupt end.

kate thompson

lives in Ireland, where she writes novels for children and young adults. She has been awarded the Bisto Book of the Year Award three times by Children's Books Ireland. Her book *The New Policeman* won the 2005 Whitbread Children's Book Award.

Also look for

Origins,

**the thrilling final installment
in the Missing Link Trilogy**

In the secret community of Fourth World, where through genetic experiments animals can talk and children have animal genes, an unimaginable alien presence appears. Vividly described by Christie in his diary, this creature raises terrifying questions. Could it be a threat to all civilized life? Alternating with the diary is the story of Nessa and Farral, young people from warring Cat and Dog tribes. Can a dangerous journey heal the rift that exists between their two communities?

Page by page, readers will uncover the connection between these two extraordinary stories, discovering what really happened when a group of scientists and misfits attempted to unravel the secrets of the missing link.